Making the Rules

Emma Leigh Reed

Other Books by
EMMA LEIGH REED

Breaking the Rules

A Fine Line

A Time to Heal

Second Chances

Trusting Love

Mirrrored Deception

EMMA LEIGH REED

Making the Rules

ELRpublishing

This book is a work of fiction. Names, characters, events, places and incidents are either products of the author's imagination or are used in a fictitious manner. Any resemblance to actual persons, living or dead, or actual events is purely coincidental.

Text copyright © 2019 by Emma Leigh Reed
All rights reserved.

No part of this book may be reproduced, or stored in a retrieval system, or transmitted in any form or by any means, electronic, mechanical, photocopying, recording, or otherwise, without express written permission from the author.

Published by ELR Publishing.

ISBN-13: 978-1-944550-10-3

Cover and interior design by Kenny Holcomb
kennyholcombdesigns.com

Printed in the United States of America

Making the Rules

one

Isabelle

"Are you freaking kidding me?" I stood at the open door to my apartment, exhaustion pulling at me. All I wanted was a hot shower and to crawl into my bed. Instead I stared at the cushions from the couch scattered about. Pictures broken and glass shards littering the carpet. I'm not sure how much time passed before reality seeped into my brain. Who would do this? What the...

I backed away from the door and reached in my purse for my cell phone. I punched in 9-1-1 as I stared at my apartment. Letting the dispatcher know that my apartment had been broken into, and that there seemed to be no damage to the door, I was told to wait outside until an officer arrived. I stayed on the phone making small talk with the dispatcher, waiting for what seemed an eternity before an officer arrived on the scene.

"Miss, this is your apartment?"

"Yes, sir. Isabelle LaFayette." I answered.

"Officer Terrell." He waited for me to continue.

"I just arrived home and when I unlocked the door, I found the mess."

"Stay here." He pushed opened the door and ventured into the house. "All clear, come on in."

I pulled my suitcase in and placed it against the wall.

"How long have you been gone?" Officer Terrell pulled his small notebook from his shirt pocket.

"A week."

"Take a look around and see if you can determine if anything is missing."

I took a slow look around the living room. Other than pictures being smashed and the couch cushions on the floor, nothing was missing. The television still sat on the stand in the corner. I moved to the kitchen and stopped just inside the doorway. I had been eclectic in my choice of kitchenware, with most of it coming from thrift shops, but almost all the dishes and glasses were smashed on the floor.

Tears caught in my throat as I looked around. Who would do this to me? I turned and went to the bedroom. The bed was untouched, but my clothes from the closet were strewn over the floor. The box where I had kept my poems from college and Jack's pictures was torn apart. The poems shredded. Thankfully, I had taken Jack's pictures with me or I would have lost those, too.

"Miss?"

I shook my head. "No, nothing seems to be missing."

"There isn't any damage to the door. Does anyone else have a key to your apartment?"

"No, no one." Anxiety pulled at me. How could I sleep here tonight? "What about the balcony?"

"It wasn't tampered with either. In fact, the bar is still

Making the Rules

in the track." Officer Terrell stood at the door. I could feel his gaze on me as I bent down and picked up a few pieces of my poetry. I would not cry over this. It was just papers and the most important things to me, I had carried with me to New Hampshire.

"Is it safe to stay here tonight?" I stood and turned towards the officer.

"I believe so. I would change the lock on your door though, just in case."

Isabelle frowned. "Do you have any recommendations at this time of night?"

"I can call a locksmith that I have used who, I'm sure, can be here shortly." Officer Terrell replied.

I nodded and he moved to the living room to make his call. I sat on my bed and just surveyed the room. With a sigh, I stood and started picking up the clothes and hanging them back in the closet. There didn't seem to be any damage to the clothes themselves.

"Miss, he'll be here within thirty minutes."

"Thank you."

"I'm just going to look around the complex here. I'll come back to check in with you before I leave to make sure the locksmith got here. His name is Adam."

I nodded and walked him to the door. I reached for my phone to call the landlord. I already knew through the lease that changing the lock was not a problem as long as I gave the landlord one of the original keys, and since there was no number for emergencies, I knew it was not a problem to get this done immediately and deal with the landlord the next day. I locked the door after him and let my head drop, closing my eyes. Immediate thoughts of how 'this is what I get for challenging my mother's attitude' towards me started flooding my mind. I shook my head. No. I wouldn't allow those thoughts to creep in. This was not my fault.

I picked up the couch cushions and straightened around the living room, taking care to pick up frames and bigger pieces of glass off the carpet. I glanced at my watch. Nine p.m. At least, it wasn't too late that it would be a nuisance if I vacuumed the place. Before pulling the machine out, I grabbed the broom from the pantry closet and swept up the kitchen floor. Once it was clean of all but the shards of glass, I went to the cupboards to look. There was a couple of plates left and one glass along with my travel coffee mug. The coffee pot was intact.

A knock at the door drew my attention away from the fact that I would need to restock my kitchen with plates and glasses. I peered through the eyehole in the door and saw a young man with a shirt that read Adam above the words Sawyer's Locksmith. I opened the door and gestured him in.

"I'm Adam." He kneeled at the door, reaching for his toolbox and a screwdriver. "Won't take but a minute, ma'am."

"Hi. Thanks for coming out on such short notice."

"Always on call to change locks in these situations. Officer Terrell thought you might like a deadbolt installed, too."

"Yes, that would be great." I turned towards my suitcase still sitting by the wall as my cell phone dinged a notification of a text message. Home yet?

Nick. I wasn't in the right frame of mind to talk to him tonight. I answered: Just got home. I'm exhausted. Talk tomorrow?

Sure

I couldn't even second guess the meaning behind

Making the Rules

the one-word answer. Was he ticked that I hadn't invited him right over? We hadn't talked my whole time in New Hampshire. I had stayed focused on what I was there to do. And emotionally draining it was, without adding more pressure to it.

"All set. Here's your new key." Adam handed me the key. I hadn't realized he was done and had packed everything away.

"Thank you. I really appreciate it."

"No problem. Have a good night." He was gone before I could respond and just as suddenly, Office Terrell was in the doorway.

"New lock already?"

I nodded and gave him a faint smile. "Everything is all set. Thank you for everything."

"Nothing seems out of the ordinary. If you hear anything, don't hesitate to call, although I'm sure someone knew you weren't home and took advantage of that. Probably were looking for money since they didn't take anything." He paused. "You going to be okay?"

"Yes. I'm fine. Just a long trip and now this. A good night's sleep will do me wonders." I gave him a sincere smile. I clicked the new lock in place on the knob and threw the deadbolt across. There was a sense of security with the click of the locks into place.

I vacuumed the living room and kitchen to make sure all the glass was up so I wouldn't have to worry in the morning about walking barefoot. I pulled my suitcase to the bedroom. I had hung up the clothes already. The rest of it…I just couldn't deal with it. I went to the bathroom, which, ironically, was spotless, just like I left it. I peeled off my clothes and turned the shower on full force. The hot water rained over me and I allowed my stress and anxiety to dissipate.

When my alarm went off, I laid there groggily as the previous night's events slowly came back. With a sigh, I pulled myself from the comfort of the bed and dressed for the day. The plan had been to arrive at work early and catch up on emails, hopefully, before Gayle arrived. Dressed to exude confidence I wasn't feeling this morning, I started the coffee maker and waited for the faithful beep so I could have my first cup of coffee. I made a mental note to look for new dishes and glassware after work.

Just as I finished getting everything together, coffee in hand and starting for the door, my cell phone beeped. I hesitated, but then ignored it. I knew it would be Nick and I just wasn't ready to face him. I hit the silence button and never gave it another thought. Arriving at work, I glanced at my watch. Six. No one would be in for a couple of hours. I loved the quietness of the office this time of the morning.

I let out a sigh of relief when I got to my desk and realized that Gayle wasn't in yet. I sipped my coffee, enjoying the warmth and familiarity of the routine as I went through emails. Not as bad as I had expected. By the time, I had finished reading and answering my emails and perusing new manuscripts that had come in, Gayle had arrived.

"Isabelle, so glad to have you back." Gayle stopped at my desk.

"Thank you. Good to be back."

"Good trip?"

I nodded. "Very good trip."

She nodded before heading into her office. "Marketing

Making the Rules

meeting in an hour," she spoke over her shoulder before she disappeared.

I pulled my phone from my bag to see that I had numerous unread text messages and five missed calls...all from Nick. Time to face the music. I read through his texts quickly, all pretty much saying the same thing. Got sucked into my emails for work. Sorry, just seeing this.

I was getting worried. Lunch today? I sighed. Could I push him off? I knew I needed to face him at some point, but I was reluctant to, and yet I couldn't put my finger on why exactly.

Meetings and working late. Didn't realize how much I would have to catch up on, I responded.

You've got to eat. He was persistent, that's for sure. Though wasn't that one of the qualities I liked?

I will at some point. I'll text you later. Meeting. My new excuse apparently was a meeting. I smiled as I put the phone in my desk drawer. I glanced at my wrist. I had some time before the marketing meeting. I opened my social media and started looking at pictures of Jack. The pictures he had online were very limited. I closed it and sat back. There was going to have to be a meeting with my favorite shrink, Mary, soon, to discuss everything that had happened.

In the meantime, work was waiting and I easily threw myself into the day. Before long it was seven at night and even Gayle was preparing to go home. I packed up my things. Take out tonight and I'll get dishes another night was one of my last thoughts before I went into acquiring mode and thinking of the newest manuscript I wanted to dive into.

two

I climbed the stairs, my laptop bag weighing heavy on my shoulder and my Chinese food in one hand. I had my keys in my other hand; my mind already making a mental list of all that needed to be done tonight. I stopped short when I came face to face with Nick standing outside my door.

"How long have you been here?" I tried to keep the irritation out of my voice.

"About a half hour. I thought I would make dinner, but looks like you already got some." He gestured towards my take-out bag.

"Yeah, I was running late by the time I left work and didn't feel like cooking."

Nick's face seemed to scowl for a moment, but it was so fleeting I thought I had imagined it. "I wanted to surprise you, but, for some reason my key isn't working, and what's with the deadbolt?"

Making the Rules

Every part of me froze in fear. Nick had a key. It came flooding back to me. I had given him a key right before I left so he could keep an eye on the place and put my mail inside. I hadn't seen any mail in the house, but I hadn't really looked for it either with the mess I had come home to.

"I had to change the locks. I came home and my apartment had been broken into." I wanted to scream at him and yet I stood outside of my apartment door wondering how I could get into my apartment and not let him in. "I'm assuming you didn't stop by with the mail while I was gone. I didn't see any." I waited for his reaction.

"Oh, my God, Isabelle. Do they know who did it?" The shock on his face seemed to be genuine enough and I felt a twinge of guilt for thinking he would have done it. He took a step towards me, but I side stepped him and unlocked the door.

"No. They said it looked like someone was looking for money since they didn't take anything really. Just a lot of smashed stuff. I just was so busy dealing with that and tired from the trip, I fell into bed to crash as soon as I could last night." I shrugged and opened the apartment door. I waited for him to answer the question about my mail.

Nick followed me into the kitchen. My nerves were frayed and I, really, just wanted to curl up with my dinner, a glass of wine, and a new book to read. "You should have called me last night. I would have come over."

"And brought my mail?" I shrugged. "I had it under control."

"We're back to that...you don't need anyone to be there for you. Well, it must have been a great reunion with Jack." The snarkiness in his voice shocked me.

"And you didn't have any mail in the week you were gone except for a couple of advertisements so I didn't bring them in."

I ignored the comment about the mail. "Reunion with Jack? What are you talking about?" I turned to look at him.

"You and I both know your real reason to return to New Hampshire was to find him."

"You are unbelievable. You know damn well Jack had nothing to do with my return to New Hampshire. For your information, not that it's any of your business, but I did not see Jack." I paused and took a deep breath. "Nick, you should go tonight. I have a lot of work to do and I'd rather be alone."

We locked eyes and, for a moment, neither of us moved. I had no idea what he was thinking, but I was praying he would just leave and not cause problems.

"You didn't see him?" His whole tone had changed, shoulders visibly relaxing.

"No." I turned back to my food and grabbed a fork from the drawer. I walked past him and sat on the couch with my dinner and started eating.

"I'm sorry, Izzy."

"Yeah. This jealousy thing you have going over a man who is no longer in my life is unreasonable. It shouldn't be a shock to you that I need time to process things." I turned the tables. I felt stronger than I had ever been since my confrontation with my parents, my aunt and father...whoever they were now.

"I think I'll go tonight." Nick walked to the door and paused.

"Good night, Nick. We can talk tomorrow, if you can be reasonable." I knew I was being bitchy by this point, but I didn't care.

Making the Rules

Without a word, Nick left the house and I let a sigh of relief escape me.

Although I knew it was late, I opened my laptop to send Mary an email.

I'm back and I think a session might be a good thing. Do you have any time soon?

I knew I wouldn't hear from her until probably tomorrow, but knowing I had taken the first step in getting back to my counselling felt good. I switched gears and opened the new manuscript that was begging to be read and settled in to finish dinner and read. I was so thoroughly engrossed in this new writer, that I was startled when my phone beeped with a new email.

Glad you're back. Tomorrow at 6 pm. Can't wait to hear how it went. ~~Mary

I smiled. There was no question as to what time would be good for me. Mary had a knack of just saying things, no nonsense. She knew I would balk if I thought about it too much, or, at least, the girl who hadn't made a trip back to New Hampshire would have. Yet, an excitement filled me with the prospect of seeing her tomorrow. I could talk through the break-in and Nick's having a key. Could he really have done it? Or was he truly shocked like he appeared? I pushed away the suspicions, knowing that, more likely than not, I was looking for an issue so I could return to being alone.

The importance of coming back to Virginia and sinking myself into my work without Nick by my side baffled even myself. Maybe it was just going to New Hampshire and having all those feelings of inadequacy come back. I shook away the negative vibes. Maybe, just maybe, after I had been back in Virginia for a while, I would go back to allowing Nick in my life again.

three

Jack

I rocked Charlotte to sleep. The poor baby had a high temperature and hadn't been keeping much down. Seeing Isabelle--Izzy--on my step earlier made my whole world stop spinning. After eight years, she looked great. But why was she there? She hadn't said anything. I smiled. Leave it to Charlotte to spit up right at that moment. I hadn't intended for her to leave when I needed to clean up, but she had walked away. Walked away, just like she had forced me to do all those years ago.

It had been years before I was able to let go of my anger at her. I realized she had pushed me away and forced me to do the only thing I could. I had wanted to marry her. Eight years. I had thought of her almost every day for the past eight years, despite all that life threw at me. And, boy there had been obstacles in my life.

After I had walked away from Izzy, I had fought against the urge to call her. I needed answers, answers I knew I

Making the Rules

would never receive. Charlotte whimpered in her sleep and I patted her back softly. This little girl in my arms was my life now. Six months ago, my life had changed forever when she came into it.

Sensing Charlotte's breathing deepen and even out, I laid her gently in the crib. As I stood over her, I smiled. Izzy would have been a great mom. Was she a mom?

I sat down in the living room, propped my feet up on the ottoman, and let my thoughts drift away to the past, as they did regularly. My life over the past few years had been a challenge, to say the least.

The memories came flooding back. My first marriage had been a bust and I had sworn I wouldn't get myself into another marriage that wasn't full of love and mutual desire. The day my divorce was final, I felt a sense of freedom, a weight that had been lifted from my shoulders. The only thing I had ever wanted in life was to love someone fully and have that love returned. I thought I had found that with Isabelle. My God. Seeing her on my doorstep this morning had thrown me. I had wanted to pull her into my arms and just ask her why. Why had she pushed me away? Why was she standing there in front of me?

I shook the thoughts of Izzy from my mind and concentr-wwated on my current situation. I met Madde and immediately had felt a connection with her. We meshed and, seemingly, wanted the same things from life. Six months after knowing each other, I felt it was time to move to the next step and proposed. She had accepted before I had finished the question. It was a whirlwind planning of a wedding, which thankfully was small and intimate. Life was good for a couple of months, until Madde started pushing to get pregnant.

I had wanted kids, but never was in a rush. I agreed with Madde so quickly because I wanted to make her happy. Instead, after six months and still no luck, we started the process of testing to see where issues may or may not lie. I was prepared to be supportive of any issues Madde might have, but when it turned out I was the one who was unable to have kids, Madde was not so supportive. Less than a year into our marriage, and the breakdown started. Instead of the life trial bringing us closer, it tore us apart. There was no thought of other options. Madde was stuck on wanting her own child. I had hoped, even prayed, that she would change her mind so we could still be parents through adoption, but she was stubborn on that front.

Then came Charlotte, and I didn't even think about it. Without a second thought, I took the little girl who needed a mother and father into my life, Madde's life, and our marriage. But if the truth be told, it never crossed my mind that Madde would be so angry at an innocent baby because of it; I thought Charlotte's presence in the home would change her mind.

"Jack?"

I opened my eyes and saw Madeline in the doorway. "I must have dozed off. Charlotte's in bed, sleeping, finally."

She nodded and crossed over to sit on the couch. "Jack, what are we going to do?"

I shook my head. "Not now. Madde, just let it go for right now. Charlotte's been really sick and I'm just wiped out. I'm going to bed."

"You always do this. It always has to be on your time-line." Madde's voice rose an octave.

"Don't you dare start so you wake her up. We both know it won't be you who soothes her back to sleep. You'll go to bed and ignore that precious little girl in there."

She stood and looked like she was going to let loose -- the familiar rant of how much I loved the child more than

Making the Rules

I did her, but instead, she just glared at me before heading to the bedroom. The door shut with a resounding thud...at least quieter than I had expected, but enough that I heard the soft cries start from Charlotte's room.

I sighed. It was going to be another long night. I rubbed Charlotte's back as I leaned over the crib, giving her just enough touch that she settled. She hadn't fully woken up and maybe, just maybe, I would be able to get a few hours of sleep.

Madde. Madeline had no problems getting sleep these days. She refused to get up with Charlotte and adamantly refused to take care of a sick child. "Not my child" had become her mantra and I was getting very sick of it. Not her child. Nope, well, then maybe she should just walk out like everyone else did when things got rough. Sorry, Izzy. That was aimed at you. Although, in my mind, I know Izzy had made me do the walking away and, somehow, I had been okay with that. If it made it easier for Izzy, I would be the bad guy. But she broke my heart and I had yet to recover from it.

Charlotte's whimpers brought me from my thoughts and I scooped her up. Sitting in the rocking chair, I cradled the baby against me and rocked. Charlotte soon settled down. I watched her sleep, amazed at how much love I felt for this child who I had only known a short time. My heart ached for her; I longed to protect her from any hurt with a fierceness that surprised me.

four

I was exhausted. Charlotte, on the other hand, was feeling better and babbling away this morning as I held her, giving her a bottle. She kept popping it out of her mouth to give me a smile. It melted my heart. This loveable little sweetheart just needed to smile and those dimples in her pudgy cheeks would bring me to my knees. She was going to be a heartbreaker when she got older. I should start planning building a tower, now, to lock her in.

"Good morning, Madde." Madde had walked past to the kitchen without a word. Oh, was this getting old, her wounded attitude.

"Morning," she finally mumbled.

"When are you going to stop this attitude?" Charlotte reached out a hand towards Madde. I waited to see if she would respond, and again I was disappointed as she ignored the sweet baby.

"I wanted to talk about it last night, but you didn't

Making the Rules

want to. And once again, we are on your timeline so I'm the bad guy because I don't want to talk about it now."

"I was tired and yet you woke her up with your slam of the bedroom door last night. It was me who stayed up with her, not you."

Madde glared at me. "Not my child."

"Yes, you keep reminding me. You wanted a child, remember?" I picked Charlotte up to my shoulder to pat her back. "You begged me to have a child."

"Yes, our child. And then we couldn't. I certainly didn't want to raise someone else's child." The coolness of her words washed over me.

"If we are raising her, it is our child." I couldn't fathom the venom that was coming from her mouth, aimed at a child barely six months of age. It wasn't Charlotte's fault that she was sitting here in my lap, a consequence of someone else's mistake. Charlotte, herself, was not the mistake and I would give my last breath to make sure this little girl knew love.

"You didn't have to take her in…and without asking me." Madde's voice projected the hurt she had been holding in for the past six months.

"Is that the problem? I didn't ask you about bringing Charlotte home? You're angry at a baby because you weren't put first in the decision? You weren't put ahead of an infant's needs?" Anger rose in me. "How selfish are you going to be? When will you ever think of anyone, but yourself?"

Madde glared at me. "Me, selfish? That's rich, Jack. You and your damn soft heart. You'd take in every stray if you could. This child was not your responsibility, but you do anything for your niece, so here she is. Look in a mirror, if you want to see selfish."

I had had it with the conversation. I placed Charlotte in her swing and gave her a toy. Upon turning towards Madde, I saw a look of pain cross her face before she neutralized her expression and said "You have no idea how I feel or think. You consider it selfish on my part. I consider it selfish on yours. I see how you look at that child."

"What?" I replied.

"You wanted your own child and you now have one. And lucky for you, you didn't need me to get it."

Of all the idiotic things to say. I was speechless and just stared at her. She threw me a withering look before she turned and left the house. Two years of marriage seemed like eternity when it was with a person that you had no idea who they really were. Madde and I seemed to hit it off at the beginning, but when the real-life things hit us, we found out very quickly how different we were in our way of handling obstacles. Marrying, after knowing Madde only six months, obviously, wasn't enough time to get to know her, truly get to know her.

I was baffled by the pain in Madde's eyes when I caught her looking at Charlotte when she thought I couldn't see her, but it was there. Yet, she wanted nothing to do with her, or me for that matter. Was she afraid that Charlotte would come between me and her? Life had done that long before the baby arrived.

If I was being honest, I loved the days when I worked at home, Charlotte playing in the background and Madde gone from the house. Life seemed almost normal, except I missed Izzy. I shook my head. No, I would not go there.

It's true. I have a soft heart and when my niece told me about her friend being pregnant and not being able to keep the child, I jumped at the opportunity to help her out. It was unconventional, but not unheard of, for a

Making the Rules

private adoption to take place. When my niece called to tell me that the baby was born, my first thought was how I wanted to share this moment with Izzy. Find out what her thoughts were, what would she do. Ironically, Madde's opinion never entered my mind and she was right about that, I never even consulted her. She had come home from work to find me holding Charlotte, and a pile of baby things on the couch. The cruel irony of it was Izzy, who couldn't talk to me when I needed her to, was the one person I wanted to talk to more than anything about life's challenges.

I sat to check my emails. I had been waiting for an email from Neil, my best friend, who, after I had left the service, brought me onboard with his company in flipping houses. I had put a tidy nest egg away in doing this for the past few years. Neil had started in real estate and found all these small, run-down houses that we had been flipping and selling for a hefty profit. Unbeknownst to Madde, I had been splitting my profits between our joint account and a separate personal account. I wasn't sure why I felt the need to do this, but after my first marriage ended, I had this niggling thought to keep a safety net for myself just in case.

I glanced over at Charlotte in her swing, content as ever. She was an easy baby, that was for sure. I pulled up my emails and there it was. We've got it was in the subject line and I clicked on it. A new-to-the-market house that was extremely run down and possibly would need to be leveled, Neil had acquired. He had paid a bit more than we normally would have liked to, but he felt, with the elderly lady who was living there, that she deserved a bit more to get her into the assisted living place.

I replied regarding arrangements to go through the

place the next day and see what exactly needed to be done. I loved this job as it gave me the flexibility of being home with Charlotte when I needed to be. My sister or my niece had no problem watching her when I needed to be on the job site for the day. It had been an ideal situation before Charlotte came into my life, but even more so, now that she was here. Madde never understood the job and thought it was unethical, stating we were taking advantage of people by buying their run-down houses, fixing them and selling them for a profit. She didn't have much of a business mind and it had led to many arguments.

I looked at the next email. I had, on a whim, sent an email to a counselor who had been recommended to me. Neil had seen, first-hand, the shambles my marriage was in after Charlotte entered the picture, and he had been the one to whom I vented my frustration about the hands-off attitude Madde had. He had seen this counselor himself and highly recommended him. The man had set up an appointment for me to meet with him on Wednesday, only a couple of days away. Maybe, just maybe, I would finally be able to make some sense of my life and where I had ended up. It wasn't a bad spot, just not where I thought I would be.

• • •

The next morning was sunny and Charlotte definitely was back to her happy-tempered self. I dropped her off at my sister's before heading to the newly acquired house. Pulling up in front of the ranch-style home, my heart sank. This was the worst of everything we had done in the past and I was only seeing the outside. I couldn't imagine what the inside looked like.

Making the Rules

I exited the vehicle and slowly walked to the front of the house. Standing back away from the door, I took in the exterior. The clapboard siding was rotten in places and in other places, just plain broken off. From the extent of the downtrodden appearance, I would imagine the inside would be filled with water damage and, quite possibly, mold. Shutters were missing from most of the windows and what was left were hanging by, quite literally, a screw. I glanced up to the roof and saw missing shingles.

The front door opened and Neil stepped out. "About time you got here."

I smiled. "Please tell me this," I gestured to the exterior, "is the worst of it."

Neil's chuckle gave it away. "Come on. This is a challenge."

"What were you thinking?" I shook my head and walked towards the door. "Show me the inside. I'm prepared for the worst."

We stepped inside to a small foyer, whose hardwood flooring was almost black with water damage. I pointed down to it. "Mold?"

"Possibly. I wouldn't be surprised. We do have a mold problem further in."

I stared at Neil. He knew mold was nearly impossible to get rid of and would probably require a complete demolition, if it was extensive.

"Don't get that look. I know what we're in for, but look at the place and then at the plans I have for it before you give an opinion." Neil walked through a small door opening into a small room. It was no bigger than 8x10, and, yet, this was the living room. The carpet was threadbare and stained. Paint was peeling off the walls

21

with looks of what could have been wallpaper under the paint. I groaned inwardly. I could not believe Neil had actually bought this dump.

"How much land is with this place?" I asked as I stepped into the kitchen off the living room.

"Two acres, which is a good size for this section of town." Neil replied.

I nodded. The kitchen was no better than anything else I had seen so far. Cupboards had missing doors, paint was peeling and the wall behind the stove looked like it was smoke covered. I pointed to it. "Fire?"

"I don't think so. I think it's just years of smoke, soot that never has been cleaned."

I stared at him. "You've got to be kidding."

Neil shrugged. "You know these houses can be in shambles."

"Not usually to this extent. You don't usually pay for this crap and, from what you told me, you paid more than it was worth."

Neil grinned. "I couldn't leave grandma without anything."

I shook my head. "Softie" I mumbled.

The two bedrooms were worse and, at the bathroom, with one glance from the door, I turned without stepping foot into it. I headed for the back door and to the yard. It was very spacious and open. It, really, was only in need of a good mowing. "Well, finally something that is decent. Even enough room for a pool, if someone wanted." The irony of a place for a pool when the house was in such bad condition was not lost on me.

"Let's look at my plans." Neil broke through my thoughts. He pulled out the notebook he constantly carried, flipping pages until he got to the right one. "Here."

Making the Rules

He handed it to me and I glanced down. I looked up at Neil and back to the notebook. There were no numbers on the paper, but the sketch I was looking at was, obviously, a new build, three-bedroom, two-bathroom ranch. The addition of a bedroom and a bath would be a huge selling point. The living room and kitchen area was total open concept, a complete opposite from the maze inside where all the rooms were connected by a small doorless frame. The open concept would give the appearance of a large space, even if actual footage was small.

I nodded. "Okay. This looks good. What are the numbers?"

"Well…I don't have all the numbers worked out yet. Obviously, we need to completely level this place. It has too much mold in it and will, definitely, be cheaper to start from scratch. Then we can add some square footage to it to help with the resale."

"I agree." I waited. When Neil beat around the bush regarding numbers it typically meant that it was going to be more expensive.

"I worked the numbers for a rehab instead of a new build. Those numbers were well over fifty grand." Neil took a breath. "We can probably…numbers aren't final… do a new build for about a hundred grand."

I gave a low whistle. "Man…don't you think that is pretty steep?"

"I have my girl doing comp on sales around here recently." Neil's 'my girl' was his real estate girlfriend who always found him the places to buy.

"And?"

"Prelim numbers give the impression we could sell it for close to 200. It would be a huge profit."

"In this neighborhood?" I shook my head. "I don't know, man."

"Yes, in this neighborhood." Neil pointed. "Drive down the road and you will see four brand new houses that have been built. They're all capes and have sold for closer to 300. I'm telling you, this is going to be a good turn around, especially if we can do it within six to eight weeks."

"Are you insane? That kind of timeline for a demolition and rebuild?"

Neil grinned. "Challenge accepted."

"You better be starting today then." I turned towards the house.

"Crew will be here tomorrow for demo. It won't take long." Neil clapped me on the back. "We've got this."

five

Isabelle

I entered Mary's outer office and hesitated for a brief second before knocking on her open door.

"Come on in, Isabelle."

Taking my usual spot by her window overlooking the ocean, the silence was palpable today. I knew she was waiting for me to start. I turned and made my way to a chair. "Where to start?"

She smiled. "Anywhere you want."

I nodded. "The trip was good. It was great to see my grandparents." I knew I was purposely shielding myself from having to tell her what had happened. Although we had talked about how I was going to handle the confrontation when I went to New Hampshire, I still wasn't in an emotional place to talk about it.

"You needed to spend some time with them. I'm sure they were a huge comfort to you." She watched me, waiting for me to confirm this. "And did you see your parents?"

I looked at the floor. "Yes." I switched gears, protecting my vulnerability over family issues. "And when I arrived home, my apartment had been destroyed."

A look of shock passed over Mary's face before her cool demeanor slipped back into her place. "Do they know what happened or who did it?"

"No. There was no forced entry. The police officer asked if anyone had a key."

Mary nodded. "And did you tell them?"

I looked at her like she had two heads. "Tell them what? About Nick having a key? No, I honestly forgot I had given him one until he showed up last night and was complaining about not being able to get in. I had changed the locks."

Mary cocked her eyebrow at me. "And?"

"The funny thing is I really don't want to deal with that right now. He's acting very jealous and…I don't know what, but I certainly don't care to be around that."

"Okay." Mary sat back and didn't say another word.

Silence took over the room. I crossed and uncrossed my legs, fidgeting in my seat. Standing, I crossed over to the window. "What am I missing?" I glanced at her.

Mary just shook her head. "Why don't you want to be around him? I thought, before you left for New Hampshire, things were going great between you two."

"They were. I just feel different now that I'm back." I wracked my brain trying to think.

"How so?" Mary prodded.

"I don't know. I feel stronger, more confident in myself and how to handle things. But somehow I still don't want anyone in my apartment right now."

"Why do you think that is?"

Making the Rules

"I guess, because I stood up to my mother." I shrugged, trying to brush off thinking too deeply about it.

Mary made a note on her pad of paper. "I thought you had gotten past all that."

"I did…I don't know. I know that I have been keeping Nick at arm's length since I got back, but some of it may be the break-in, and getting back to work. It was an emotionally exhausting trip to begin with." The words just tumbled out.

"Well, let's talk about the trip to New Hampshire. Did you see Jack?"

"I confronted my parents on not being my parents. To this day my mother still continues to say my suicide attempt was just a moment of not feeling good." Bitterness laced my words. "And, I am comfortable with my decision to cut her out of my life."

"You mention your mother, but not your father. Does he feel the same way about the suicide attempt as she does?"

I shook my head. "No. I think he just didn't want to cause waves." I made my way back to the chair. "She's not my mother…but he's my father."

"Excuse me?" Mary looked up from her pad of paper.

"Yeah, apparently, my father got my mother pregnant…the sister of the woman who raised me."

"Well, that's a mouth full. How do you feel about that?"

I curled my leg up under me. "Really? That's such a shrink question."

Mary laughed. "I am a shrink, as you say."

"I was thrown when my dad told me that. And pissed off. If he was always my father, and knew it, why didn't he stand up for me when she was berating me and belittling me at every turn?"

"Only he can answer that." Mary answered.

"I know. But what about me? I was an innocent child. She acted like she hated me just because she was mad that she was raising her sister's child...although she didn't know it was actually her husband's child too." The absurdity of the whole situation hit me. Laughter just rolled out of me and I couldn't stop. Tears rolled down my cheeks as Mary just stared at me. Finally getting myself under control, "Sorry. It's just so..."

"I understand. It's a situation you have no idea how to handle. It's stressful and you hurt from it. Laughter is a way of letting that out, for a moment. You have to deal with this, Isabelle."

I shook my head. "Not now I don't. I need to deal with the break-in at the apartment."

"That seems pretty minor, doesn't it, considering all the other scenarios in your life you are dealing with?"

"I was violated. My home was destroyed, dishes shattered, pictures broken. My poems I had written ripped into pieces." I trailed off and slumped back into the chair. It was so easy to focus on this instead of anything else. Mary knew me so well.

"Yes, you were. But who would have done this?"

"I don't know, honestly." I glanced at my watch.

"Yes, it's time." Mary chuckled. "Just when the conversation is getting hard, you get to escape."

I grinned at her.

"The time to stop self-deflecting will come soon." Mary spoke as I was leaving. I raised my hand in a wave as I walked out.

six

The week flew by as I threw myself back into work. Within four days, I had pitched two new books to Gayle and she had agreed to acquire both of them. I was excited to work with these new authors. I had a renewed sense of purpose with my job and realized that, although I enjoyed the week off, slipping back into being a workaholic was easier than I anticipated. Friday arrived in a flurry of activity between meetings at work and still trying to catch up from the week's vacation I'd had.

Nick and I hadn't spoken much since that night I had asked him to leave. It dawned on me Friday that, although we had been close and he had even told me he loved me before I left for New Hampshire, there had been no physical touch between us since I returned--no kiss, no hug. Since that first night, he had text me very little. The ball was in my court, I supposed, but work was utmost on my mind.

I was just leaving work for the weekend when my phone beeped. You back? Drinks? I smiled. Diane and I had become fast friends and I could use a girls' night to chat.

Definitely. Flamingo's?

In 30. Diane was less of a texter than I was. Her one to two-word answers always brought a smile to my face. I would have time to run home and change into something comfy before heading to the bar.

Diane had arrived first. I caught her waving to get my attention as I walked through the door. I made my way to the bar. The place was standing room only already tonight. Friday nights were busy, but I expected something a bit quieter so early in the evening. Diane had already ordered two margaritas for us.

"There was a couple of empty tables outside." I spoke as I reached her. She handed me my drink and nodded. We made our way back through the crowd and found an empty table outside.

"Finally. That place is mobbed." Diane shook her head. "Maybe I'm just getting old, but the party scene this early in the evening doesn't excite me anymore."

I laughed. "I don't know about old, just a change of perspective. I don't remember ever being out drinking all night like these kids do now."

"You're an old soul, apparently. Did you not have your rebellious days of going against your parents?" Diane had no idea how close that statement hit home.

"Not with drinking and partying. They were pretty strict." I sipped my drink and allowed the stress of the week to wash away. The sounds of the waves against the pier's pilings was soothing. We sat in silence, each of use sipping our drink.

Diane finally broke the silence. "Well, you going to tell me about your trip?"

Making the Rules

I set my drink down on the table. "It was good."

"Hmm. That's a vague answer. Come on, details, girl. Did Nick miss you terribly?"

I sat forward. "That's the odd thing. He's been irritable and just acting weird. Of course, I've been distracted and not been paying attention. The night I got home, my apartment had been broken into and trashed."

"What? Are you kidding?"

"I wish I was. Most of my dishes and glasses shattered on the floor, all my clothes were pulled from the closet and tossed around my room, although they weren't damaged." I thought back to my first view of the mess. It was very deliberate, really. The bathroom was untouched, living room not really destroyed, other than my pictures and then it was just the glass in the frames that was broken. It was the kitchen where the real damage was done, and my cigar box that held my poetry…and used to hold my pictures of Jack and me.

"I can't believe you are sitting here so calm about it." Diane's voice broke into my thoughts.

"I know, right? I guess, although it was a mess, it didn't feel like an immediate threat. The police thought someone realized I was gone and was just looking for money. Nothing was taken."

"Could be, I suppose. Have you been staying there?"

I nodded. "Changed the lock that night and the locksmith installed a deadbolt too."

"What did Nick say?"

"I didn't call him that night, and in fact when he texted me I told him I was tired and just going to bed. I never mentioned it to him until he said his key wasn't working when he tried to get in to make dinner before I got home one night."

Diane sat back. "How did that happen?"

"What?"

"What's going on that you didn't even think to tell him, or that you deliberately didn't tell him. I thought things were good with you two."

I shrugged and finished my drink. I signaled to the waitress that we wanted two more before I turned back to Diane. "I don't know. I really don't. He's acting weird and, maybe I'm just on edge because of the break-in, but I can't put my finger on it."

Diane stared at me. "Izzy, what happened in New Hampshire?"

"You know the issues with my parents, not being listed on my birth certificate. We had a confrontation. I guess I let years of suppressed anger and hurt out. It felt great and I found out about my birth mother. My grandparents finally told me everything and gave me letters she had written to me."

"Okay." Diane dragged the word out a bit. "So that's good stuff. Why the sudden distance from Nick?"

I shook my head as the waitress came over with our drinks. "I don't know. Maybe I'm just too emotionally wiped out to deal with a man." I laughed, trying to force lightness into the conversation. "Tell me what you've been doing while I was gone."

"Nothing exciting. Same shit, different day." Diane paused for a sip of her drink. "I have met this new guy."

"Nothing exciting? Really? Spill the details, girl." I sat forward.

"Nothing to tell, really. We had dinner a couple of times. I met him at a work function. He seems nice. There just isn't that spark, you know?"

"The elusive spark." I laughed. "I don't think it really exists."

Making the Rules

"Right! What is it with men thinking they are so attracted to you right off?" Diane pondered. "Or what am I missing?"

"I hear ya. I feel the same thing. My first thought is, it must be me. And, of course, you and I are quite alike."

Diane raised her glass. "To standing on our own and not looking for the unicorn."

We clicked glasses. "Amen to that."

The evening flew by and, by the time we were ready to call it a night, Diane knew every detail of my trip and had been sworn to secrecy. I walked home along the beach, shoes in my hand, ankle-deep in the ocean. The cool water swirling around my legs with every wave that came rolling in, washing the stress away. My mind was free, at least for the moment, from the stressors of my returning to Virginia. I love my job, but how often in the past week had I wondered if I really fit in here? Did I need to move somewhere else and start again? Damn, how many times did I have to start over to feel a sense of belonging somewhere?

I knew the answer to that, but I didn't like it. Or maybe it was the alcohol making me wish for something that wasn't there. As hard as I tried to block my thoughts away from Jack, I couldn't. He was still there. My heart and soul still belonged to him. I knew this. The reason, probably, that I was never going to allow Nick into my heart. I have always known that, but I allowed the friendship and company. It fulfilled a basic need for me, but the reality was, I would never love him.

I also knew that Jack was never going to be a part of my life. It was not even a remote possibility at this point. Could I force myself to move on and force myself to pretend to love Nick? Could I fake it until it was real? Would it ever be real if I pretended at first? Talking with Diane had sparked in me the need for not settling for something that wasn't there just because I needed to move on from Jack. I shook my head and headed for the street and my apartment building across from me. One thing was for sure, life was going to continuing to throw surprises at me. I only prayed that I would be able to handle them with the confidence I'd had in New Hampshire…at least, on this recent trip.

seven

Saturday brought dark and dreary skies with the threat of rain. Since it was not raining yet, I sat on my balcony with a blanket around me watching the waves pounding the beach. The darkness loomed ahead of me as I watched the black clouds roll in over the horizon. It would be only a matter of time before the driving rains would come and I would be forced to withdraw inside for the day.

Today I wasn't in the mood for reading new things or even editing someone's work. I wanted a down day. I wanted to contemplate life and think about moving. Did I really? Where would I go? Why would I leave the job I had now? Was I feeling this way because of the break-in and, underneath, I truly felt unsafe here?

A knock on the door brought my out of my ruminations. There was Nick, flowers in hand. Yellow roses in a blue cobalt vase. He knew they were my favorite. I sighed. "They're beautiful."

"I'm truly sorry for the other night, Izzy. I don't know what came over me."

"Me, too. Come on in." I placed the vase on the side table in the living room. "Let's just forget it. I think we both were feeling some stress from things going on."

"I think we should talk about your trip to New Hampshire."

"No." I was surprised at the sharpness in my voice. "I've talked enough about New Hampshire. How about a movie day and we just relax?"

I could tell Nick wasn't happy with my answer, but he smiled at me and nodded. "Action or chick flick?"

I wasn't in the mood for a sappy love story. "Action, definitely."

I popped some popcorn and grabbed a couple of beers from the fridge while Nick perused the movie channel. We agreed on a Jason Statham movie and settled in with our snacks and a blanket. The next two hours flew by as we were engrossed in the movie. I was thankful for the mindlessness of just watching TV. As the credits rolled by, I felt myself tense up. What now? It was still late morning and already I was ready for the day to be over.

"How about some lunch?" Nick asked.

"Are you really hungry after the popcorn? I don't think I could eat."

"You say that now, but once food gets in front of you, you never seem to have any trouble putting it away." Nick snickered.

"Funny, although, usually, true." I relented. "What were you thinking?"

"It has started pouring so I'm not sure I really want to go out in it. Order a pizza?" Nick reached for his cell phone.

Making the Rules

"That works. Get what you want. I probably will only eat one piece."

We were looking for another movie to watch while waiting for the pizza to arrive. I figured if I picked up in the kitchen, I could avoid any unwanted conversation. No such luck I realized as I heard Nick clear his throat behind me.

"Izzy?"

"Yeah." I turned to face him.

"I really want to talk about this." Nick, although casually leaning against the wall, seemed so unsure of himself. A pang of guilt hit me that I was, maybe, being a bit unfair to him.

"Talk about what?"

"I acted like a jackass the other night. I'm sorry. You're right. I'm jealous of a man you aren't even in contact with."

I sighed. "I thought we got past this long before I even went to New Hampshire. Things were good until this trip."

"I know. I want to go back to that." Nick walked toward me.

"I can't deal with the jealousy. Jack isn't here."

"Not even in your mind?" He stopped right in front of me, but not touching me.

"I can't forget memories of anything in my past, Nick. I don't ask you to forget your memories. I'm sure you have had other girlfriends who you think of every once and awhile." I tilted my head to look him in the eyes.

"You're saying you only think of him once and awhile?" Nick questioned.

I prayed my face stayed neutral. "Yes. He isn't a constant in my thoughts." I hated lying about Jack, but I couldn't tell Nick how I still thought of Jack daily and how Jack always came to mind when there was something good or bad that happened and I wanted to share with him.

Nick reached for me and pulled me into his arms, holding me close. He whispered, "God, Izzy, I was afraid I had lost you."

I allowed my arms to tighten around him to reassure him. "We're good. Don't worry."

A knock at the door broke us apart and Nick went to grab the pizza. I let out my breath, not realizing I had been holding it. Things had been good before the trip. There was no reason we couldn't get back to that. I thought of the yellow roses. He brought my favorite flower. Things could work out. I grabbed a couple of paper plates and headed back to the living room.

"What's next for a movie?"

"I suppose you're wanting a sappy love story?" Nick looked at me.

I shook my head no. "I'd prefer comedy or action."

"I knew there was a reason I loved you." Nick starting flicking through the choices of comedy movies.

I, internally, winced at the words. Why, oh why, must he bring that word into it? I berated myself for the thought and tried to let it go. Chill and movies. By tonight, I would be ready to dive back into manuscript reading.

By the time the afternoon had passed, and we had watched three movies, I was ready to call it a day, but Nick appeared to be settled in for the long haul, and I tried to stifle a yawn.

"Tired? Want some coffee or we could take a nap instead?" Nick asked.

"I'm a bit tired, but coffee, it has to be. I have a ton of work to get to and I've already wasted most of the day."

Making the Rules

Nick scowled. "Watching movies with me is a waste of time?"

"I didn't mean it like that. But I'm still trying to catch up from taking time off. I have a lot to do."

"Go ahead and do it." Nick started flipping channels and stopped on a baseball game.

After making coffee, I grabbed a cup and my laptop and headed to the bedroom. Propping myself up with pillows behind me, I opened my laptop and started to work. I found myself lost in a mystical fantasy story. The uniqueness of the plot and characters pulled me in. I found myself drifting into the abyss of a new world and losing all sense of time of the real one.

As I reeled and pillaged my way through the book, I mentally cheered for the protagonist who was finding her way on her own and swore at her to watch out when the villain was sabotaging her. The story had me so enthralled I didn't realize the time and was yanked from my imagination when Nick laid on the bed next to me.

"Game over?" I asked, trying to go back to the story.

"Yup. You about done with your stuff?"

I shook my head no. "Only about half way through it." My eyes stayed on the screen, and I was trying to refocus on the words, but the moment of pure bliss of being inside another's story was gone. With a sigh, I snapped my laptop closed and looked at Nick.

"Am I interrupting?" I could tell by the expression on his face, he knew full well he was interrupting me.

"Yes, but I guess I can take a small break and finish up a bit later."

The subtle meaning Nick recognized immediately and his smiled faded. "After you kick me out for the night?" His tone was harsh and I watched him.

"Why are you suddenly so irritable?" I sat up straight.

"I just feel like you're still pushing me away, Izzy. Why don't you just give me a new key and let me stay."

I internally winced at the idea of giving him a new key. "I don't have any extras made up right now. I'll try and get that done this week." I tried to brush it off and hoped he would accept that.

He didn't say anything, but moved my laptop to the side and pulled me down next to him on the bed. His body laid across part of mine, just enough weight to hold me still unless I really wanted to move. I waited.

"Izzy." He murmured as his lips grazed mine before the kiss became more demanding, almost possessive. I tried to pull back, but he had moved his hand to the back of my head, rendering me nearly immobilized. I pushed against him. "What?"

"What is up with you?" I pushed him away. "This isn't like you, so forceful."

"You like forceful. I remember a night you told me it was exactly what you needed." Nick sat up on the bed not even trying to hide his irritation.

"Not like this. My God, Nick, you act like you have to prove something." I stood and picked up my laptop and coffee cup and headed for the kitchen.

"Well, you do what you do best and just run away from anything that requires a conversation."

I turned in the doorway. "I'm not running away. This is my house."

"You are so quick to point out all of a sudden. Your house, you can handle things. Why do you bother to keep me around, Izzy?" The condescending tone was enough to send me over the edge.

"Nick, don't push your luck. Ever since I got back you

Making the Rules

have been irritable, possessive and jealous. Not one of those traits is attractive. If you want things to go back to the way they were, look in a mirror and at your behavior. Or, if you don't like it, why bother to stay at all?" I turned and walked out of the room.

I stood by the kitchen table, shaking. I was furious... at Nick and at myself. Why was I letting this bother me? I know he suddenly needs reassurance, but, damn it, the kiss felt forced and I would not be forced to do anything I didn't want to.

The shutting of the apartment door drew my attention and I returned to the living room to find Nick gone. "Nick?" I peeked into the bedroom. He was definitely gone. I walked to the door and flicked the deadbolt into place and double-checked to make sure the other lock was secure. A feeling of uneasiness settled over me and I walked to the balcony to look outside. The rain had slowed to a steady drizzle. There was no sign of Nick outside that I could see from the balcony.

I pulled the curtains shut and paced around the living room. My nerves were frayed and suddenly I didn't want to be alone in the house. I reached for my cell phone and punched in Diane's number.

"Hey girl, what's up?" Diane's sprightful voice was a comfort.

"Hey, what are you doing tonight?" I jumped right to it.

"No plans. Just hanging out. Want to do something?" Diane asked.

"I hate to invite myself, but could I spend the night at your place?" I bit my bottom lip as I waited for her answer.

"Of course. What happened though, or you want to wait until you're here to talk about it?"

"We'll talk when I get there. Let me throw some stuff together and I'll be there shortly."

eight

Jack

I parked outside the building and took a deep breath. I had planned on doing this for years, and I just couldn't put it off any longer. I needed someone to talk to, about everything, without walking on eggshells. I was tired of carrying the weight of the world on my shoulders with no help. This was it. The moment of truth. I had finally broken down to see a counselor. He had come highly recommended from Neil, but I still wasn't sure about this. I made my way to the door. Charles Winham. Bold, clean letters on the doorway let me know I was in the right place.

A sign just inside on a small stand caught my eye. Please take a seat. I'll be with you in a moment. Must be in with someone still. I found a chair and flipped through a magazine. The pages were a blur and I couldn't concentrate on what was in front of me. In my mind, I ran through things that needed to be talked about...things I didn't really want to talk about. Why was I here? I wasn't

Making the Rules

sure this was the best thing for me, but at this point, my life needed something…something more than it had now.

Not more than five minutes had passed when the inside door opened and a teenage boy came out. He scowled at me and was gone before I could say a word.

"Mr. Riley?" The voice from the doorway brought my attention to the man standing there. A 60-something year old with a close grey beard and wire-rimmed glasses. He was right out of a book…which book, I couldn't say.

"Yes." I stood and put out my hand to shake his.

"Come on in." He stepped back and I entered his office. The room was decorated with dark wood and leather. A black leather couch and two matching arm chairs were in the center of the room. On the far wall was a mahogany desk with a laptop and a single lamp. The other walls held floor to ceiling bookcases, filled with books. The only disorder in the office came from the bookshelves. "Have a seat."

I chose one of the arm chairs and continued to look around. Finally settling my gaze on him, I realized he was watching me with a pad of paper in his lap, a pen laying on top of it. "Please call me Jack."

"Jack, it is. What brings you to see me?"

Well, there it was. Right out there. No small talk. I supposed there shouldn't be small talk at the price I was paying per hour. I took a breath. "I just…" I just what? I had no words to describe what it was I thought I needed.

"You just?" He prompted.

"I'm not sure." I sat back feeling defeated. My life was a train wreck and all I could come up with was I'm not sure.

"Well, tell me a little bit about yourself. Married?"

I nodded. "A second marriage, yes."

"Okay. How long have you been married?"

43

I sighed. I wanted to say eternity, but opted for the actual length. "Two years."

He must have heard the dejection in my voice, "not going well, huh?" His question was quiet, and more of an observation than a real question, but it made me think.

"Define well." I let out a small laugh.

"Still in the honeymoon phase?" He raised an eyebrow at me, knowing the answer before I could shake my head no.

"Not even close."

He nodded. "Let's start there then."

"I don't even know where the beginning is really. We met, seemed to hit it off, then realized we handle life challenges a bit differently. Since then we just seem to co-exist."

"What life challenges have you viewed differently? Two years of marriage isn't a lot of time to see a lot of challenges, I wouldn't think."

He was right. Two years shouldn't have been a long time. It should have been fun, loving, full of passion. "She wanted children and I couldn't give her one. At least not in the conventional way. I'm now a guardian to the sweetest baby girl and Madde will have nothing to do with her."

Charles held up his hand. "Let's go back a little further. How soon after marriage did you try to start a family?"

"Right after we got married. Madde wanted a baby within the first year and started pushing to begin trying within a couple of months after the wedding. I wasn't against it, but I didn't want to rush into it. Either way, it was taken out of our hands when she couldn't get pregnant and then, after some doctor's appointments, it was determined that I was sterile." God, I hated that word.

Making the Rules

Charles scribbled on the paper and nodded. He never looked up from his writings, but when the pen paused I sensed he was waiting for me to continue.

"We handled it differently. I brought up the idea of adoption or fostering children and she didn't want to do that. She stated she only wanted a child of her own, not someone else's. I wasn't comfortable with artificial insemination just so she could carry the child and it not being my child, though. Seems a bit odd to me." I paused. "It became a very sore subject so we just kind of stopped talking. The distance between us just continued to grow over the past year."

"And this child you are now guardian to, how old is this child?"

"Six months."

Charles looked up at me, his pen stopped mid-word. "Okay. And how did this come about?"

I stared into space for a few minutes, trying to formulate a politically correct response. Finally, I shrugged and just started. "My niece has a friend. They're teenagers, but her friend made a mistake and the consequence was a pregnancy. She hid it for the most part, but, when her mother found out, she informed her daughter that she couldn't come home unless she got rid of the baby. By this time, the girl was seven months pregnant. Too far along for an abortion, and at a loss on what to do. Her mother agreed for her to stay in the house, as long as her father didn't find out. They hid the pregnancy somehow and then, a few weeks before her due date, the young girl went into labor."

The words rushed out of me. I hadn't even told this to Madde. I had promised my niece and her friend that I would keep the secret of where the baby came from. "My

45

niece talked about it with me and I didn't want the child to just go anywhere." I shook my head.

"And you took the baby?"

"I met with the mother at a diner. She told me about her home situation and how she just wanted to go back home, finish high school and go to college. She was insistent that she had to give up the baby and she didn't want any contact with the baby. I made a deal with her that I would talk to a lawyer for her and have him draw up papers to make me guardian. I didn't want her to terminate all her rights."

I stood and started pacing around the room. Charles just watched me, waiting for me to continue. "We agreed I would take the baby that night and my niece would let her know what day to meet me to sign the papers. She went to the lawyer's and, before signing, she requested that I adopt her…Charlotte."

"And did you adopt her?"

"Right now, I'm her guardian, but after a year, the adoption will go through. I wanted a waiting period in case she changed her mind."

"So, Madde, your wife, didn't like that idea and you did it anyway?" Charles' question had no judgement in it, yet I felt it anyway.

"Not exactly." I sat back down. "I did it all and didn't even talk to her about it. I, honestly, didn't think about it. I brought Charlotte home that first night and Madde came home and was not happy. But I couldn't leave the infant knowing she needed a home. Honestly, I never thought about her possibly not wanting to raise her. I told her my plan of wanting to be a guardian and she never said no, she just said 'that's your deal'."

"Ahhh…and you didn't think that was a red flag to

Making the Rules

your marriage?" Charles again held no judgement in his tone, but his words hit me hard.

"My marriage, if you can call it that, was long dead before Charlotte arrived in our home." I struggled to keep the frustration out of my voice.

"Why do you stay then?"

I sighed. "Because it's the right thing to do. I have an obligation to my wife."

Charles raised an eyebrow at me. "An obligation?"

"Well, you know. Marriage vows. I can't just walk out on her."

Charles set his pad of paper aside. "I think that is a good starting point for next time. However, before we meet again I want you to really think about the word obligation and what that means to you."

I nodded, shook his hand, and the session was over. I had survived, yet there was a feeling that I wasn't going to like what was to come.

nine

Isabelle

Pulling up to Diane's bungalow, I noticed the house aglow with lights glowing from every window. Her electric bill must be outrageous. As I started up her walk, the music was blaring to the point that I doubt she would even hear the doorbell. I didn't need to worry about that considering the door flung open as soon as I reached small porch.

"I'm so glad you're here." Diane grabbed my arm and pulled me in.

"What's gotten into you?" I looked around. "Start drinking without me?"

Diane laughed. "No. I haven't been drinking at all. I was thinking we could have a small party, invite some friends over. I haven't called anyone yet. What do you think? I can call Nick and have him come, too."

"No." The word came out viciously, surprising myself and, obviously, Diane as she took a step back.

Making the Rules

"O--kay." She moved to the stereo and turned down the music. "What happened?"

I slumped onto her couch and waited for her to sit before I spilled it all out -- the way Nick had showed up with flowers, stayed even when he knew I had work to do, and even the forcefulness of the kiss and how uncomfortable it had made me.

"Wow. You don't think he would do something...I mean, he wouldn't force himself on you?"

I shook my head. "I really don't think so, but this whole jealousy act since I've gotten back is getting old and making it so I don't even want to see him."

"When he left, you didn't want to be alone though because you were feeling uncomfortable?"

"Yeah." I looked at my fingernails, playing with an imaginary hangnail.

"Hey, you did the right thing. I'm glad you called. No party. Just you and me. Girls night." Diane reached for my hand and gave it a squeeze. "This doesn't sound like Nick though."

"No. His actions have been totally out of character for him." Saying the words, I realized that was the problem. This wasn't the Nick I had grown to know and this difference was a man who I wanted nothing to do with. "What changed for him to be like this though? Did something happen while I was gone?"

"Not that I know of, but then again I don't see him that often."

I shrugged. "We're not talking about him tonight. I'll deal with that another time."

Diane laughed. "Sounds like we need some wine."

Diane refilled our wine glasses for the third time, or was it fourth...I couldn't remember at that point. We had talked about everything from our high school crushes to what we really wanted in a man. My phone had been blowing up all evening and we had been ignoring the text messages from Nick. I, with just enough alcohol in me, was ready to tell him where to go.

Diane grabbed the phone. "No. You're not going to say anything." She briefly skimmed the last text that Nick had sent before she started typing.

"What are you doing?" I reached for the phone.

"Putting an end to this tonight." She hit send and then returned the phone to me. I looked at it. There was a smiley face and then the words Can't talk. Party time

"You didn't!" I looked at her with wide eyes.

"Blah...every man needs to know that he can lose someone if he doesn't shape up. Let Nick wonder where you are, who you're with." Diane reached for the phone again and powered it down. "We're not putting our phones back on until the morning."

My head was pounding when I opened my eyes. Diane's guest bedroom was bright and the windows were on the east side so the sun was shining through brightly. I had forgotten what a hang-over headache I got from indulging in wine. The events of the night started coming back. Diane certainly did get a bit out of control with a bit of alcohol in her, and I had no problem following suit. It had felt good to let go and not think of anything or anyone for a while.

The problem was, this morning I felt like crap and everything we had done and said last night, I had a feeling, was going to come back and bite me in the ass. I heard Diane up and moving about so I figured it was time to face the music. Splashing cold water on my face and brushing my hair into a ponytail, I glanced down at the

Making the Rules

clothes I had apparently slept in. Feeling too nauseous and my head pounding, I decided it was too much effort to change my clothes.

I came into the kitchen as Diane was pulling coffee mugs out of the cupboard. She looked over at me and grinned. "Tough night?"

"Don't tell me you don't have a headache at all?"

She laughed. "I took ibuprofen before I went to bed. You, on the other hand, were insistent that taking a pain reliever before going to bed to prevent a hang-over was nothing but an old wife's tale."

I shook my head at her.

"I guess you were wrong about that." She pointed to the table where a glass of water and two ibuprofen sat waiting for me.

I stuck out my tongue at her and swallowed the pills. Closing my eyes, I willed the pain relievers to work quickly. My momentary silence was interrupted by Diane, "coffee's ready". Once coffee had appropriately been digested and my head had settled down to a dull pounding, I turned toward Diane. "What did we do last night?"

"Nothing. We didn't leave the house. Sat here and drank all night and giggled like schoolgirls."

I snorted. "Schoolgirls. Is that what you called it when you were texting Nick from my phone?"

Diane looked at me. "Ummm, I forgot about that. How bad were the texts?"

"I haven't even turned my phone on yet, but I vaguely remember you saying something about a party."

Diane started laughing. "That's right. Make him wonder what you are doing. Oh, I wonder how many times he texted you last night or called."

Not feeling at all reassured, I went to find my phone in the living room. Finally locating it under a couch cushion, I pushed on the power button and waited for it to power up. The dinging was nonstop for a good couple of minutes. I was afraid to look down at it. Thirty-three text messages and twelve missed calls with five voice mails.

"Don't read them or listen to the voice mails. Just delete everything and act like it never happened." Diane said. "If he says anything, just tell him I was using your phone and there was nothing there when you got up in the morning. He'll think I deleted everything. You probably don't want to know if he's pissed or not."

"I can't delete them without looking at them." I looked at Diane and back to the phone, but I made no effort to open the text messages or dial my voice mail.

"I'm not sure you want to know. Honestly, we can chalk it up to having a little bit too much to drink, but, if he says something in those messages that he wouldn't normally say to your face, it will be very hard to forget it."

Her logic sounded reasonable, yet I had to know. The way he had been irritable since I got back, I knew these messages weren't going to be good, but I was drawn to them. There was a need to know what he said that burned in me and I couldn't ignore it. I finally opened the text messages and looked at the long string of messages that had been left. Mostly one or two words at a time. Are you ok?, Where are you?, Izzy!?! They were really benign and more just of the nature of being worried for me.

I shrugged and showed them to Diane. "See, nothing major."

Diane snorted. "Let's wait and see what his voice mails say before you think it's nothing major."

"This is your fault, you know. If you hadn't texted

Making the Rules

him telling him it was party time, he never would have blown up my phone like this."

Diane laughed. "I'm not sure that's true. I think, from the way he's been acting, he might have done just that, regardless."

"You're impossible." I dialed the voice mail and putting the phone on speaker, I let the voice messages play.

"Message one. Izzy answer my texts."

"Message two. Where are you?"

"Message three. This is really pissing me off now. Answer the damn phone."

"Message four. Pick up the damn phone now."

"Message five. You don't want to be doing this, Izzy."

I looked at Diane. He definitely sounded pissed off. I shrugged. It's not like we were engaged or anything. I could do what I wanted and with whomever I wanted. The defiance in me was released from the depths where I had hid it away years ago. I could feel it coming out through my bones. This man…this man would not control me.

"Izz…the look on your face tells me something serious is going through your mind. Think it through before you do anything. Last night was my fault. I never should have texted Nick with your phone." Diane pleaded.

"I'm not going to do anything. I'm just not going to be controlled and treated like I'm a possession. He can either get back to the way he used to be or he can take a hike."

Diane pointed her finger at me. "Are you sure about that?"

"Look, you know about Jack. You know my heart is still his. I'm never going to fall in love with Nick. He's fun when he's not being an ass, but right now, I don't want to deal with this behavior."

"I know, but Izzy. Jack is, Jack isn't here and I don't

even know what to say about that. I have been thinking and thinking about it since we talked last, but you are not any closer to closure with him than you were eight years ago."

I nodded. "The difference is I can acknowledge the way I feel and be okay with it. It doesn't hurt anymore to say I love him still. And, as long as I'm okay with that, everything else will be the way it's supposed to be, with or without Jack in my life."

We sat there in silence, enjoying the rest of our coffee until the phone started ringing. "Guess who," Diane said as she stood up. "I'm going to go shower, give you some privacy for that conversation."

I nodded as I pushed the answer button. "Hey."

There was silence. "Hey? That's how you answer my call after all those messages I left last night?" Nick's anger was clear, but if he thought I was going to give in and allow his anger to make me complacent, he was wrong.

"There's nothing wrong with the way I answered the phone. Did you call just to be a jackass or did you actually want to talk to me?"

"What the f…" Nick stopped himself. "Izzy, I was worried last night."

"Worried, why? I gave you no reason to think I was in a position that you needed to worry about."

"I disagree, but if you want to play it that way, fine."

I was taken back by his sudden change in thought process. "I was hanging out with Diane that's all. It was no big deal."

"I was just worried." Nick's voice had softened.

I shrugged knowing he couldn't see it, but I really had nothing to say to that.

"Can we get together and talk? This time since you

Making the Rules

have been home from the trip feels like we are a million miles apart."

"Yeah, it does. But I've just had so much on my mind. It's not you. I just need some alone time to process things."

Nick grunted. "By shutting me out. Great."

"Oh, my God, get over it, would you? I don't pressure you to tell me everything." I, again, was irritated at the turn in the conversation. "I'll talk to you later."

Hanging up the phone, I stared at it in my hand. Was my patience short with Nick because of his behavior or because of the events that happened in New Hampshire? I really had only shared them with Mary and Diane, and, at this point, Diane was the only one who knew every detail.

ten

After leaving Diane's, I had found my way back to my apartment via the thrift shop to pick up some new dishes and glasses to replace the ones I had lost. I was just finishing washing them when a knock on my door startled me. Still fighting a headache from my over-indulgence the night before, I hesitated. I didn't want to see anyone. Coward, I chided myself, yet I didn't move. I listened to whoever was at the door knock a bit more insistently and then, finally, stop. I walked quietly to the living room and stood still. I heard nothing, but couldn't be sure they had gone down the stairs.

I tiptoed into the bedroom and laid down. Sleep wasn't about to come to me, I realized, after I had laid there for a while with my eyes closed and feeling wider awake than ever. I opened my eyes and looked around the room. I got up and went to the closet. Looking up at the shelf that had held the cigar box, I cringed. The

Making the Rules

fact that my poems were gone and the box that, although was nothing special, was special to me and I longed for some sense of familiarity; I missed the comfort of that box that had been with me all these years--my connection to Jack. Reaching for another box on the upper shelf, I drew it down and brought it to the bed. I may not have my original poems, but I could recreate them or write something new.

I pulled out an old notebook from the box, one that held random phrases or song lyrics. I rifled through the pages, stopping and pondering different things, letting the memories take me back. I started piecing my teen-age and college years back together through the random thoughts in the notebook. It was a dark time, yet some of the things I had written had been hopeful and showed that I wasn't completely lost in my thinking that every-thing was wrong in my life. Things picked up in the note-book when the dates coincided with the time Jack had come into my life. Hope and love filled the pages.

I came to a page where Jack's name was doodled all around. Jack Riley. The hearts that bordered the page and around his name made me smile. A foolish girl had writ-ten this. A girl who had hope that, one day, she could find happiness. A girl whose life had changed with one act, well two acts really. If I was honest, the first pivotal moment in shaping me came from the suicide attempt. An attempted suicide survivor. I hated that term. I didn't feel like a survivor, and certainly didn't back then. But then, the act of pushing Jack away before telling him I loved him had molded the way my life had gone. I had put myself on a path of self-destruction from the moment I broke my own heart.

I turned to the next blank page. I sat and stared at the page wondering where to begin. I thought back to college days during which I had spent hours writing poetry. How did I do it back then? Then it hit me. I used to think of a word or a phrase and let my thoughts take me along the path of that phrase, writing anything that came to mind. I pushed myself off the bed with my notebook and headed to the living room. Settled onto the couch, pen and notebook ready, I closed my eyes and allowed my mind to clear.

My thoughts drifted to the hope I had found in the notebook, hope that had been associated with Jack. Unfairness. The word darted into my mind and I silently said the word again and again. Unfairness. Life was unfair. Fate could be unfair. No, it wasn't fate. It was our own doing. The words tumbled over and over again through my mind. Unfair. Fate. Life changes. Growing pains. These phrases surprised me and I tried to not think too hard on them. I let my mind wander with each word that came to mind.

Peace.

I opened my eyes with that one. What was it about peace that made me feel relaxed? Was the thought of putting pen to paper giving me a second chance? A chance to pour out my emotions like I once did, to put the emotions on paper and let them go? I had stopped writing when I pushed Jack away and all those years, the emotions bottled up in me. Jack. I could still see his smile and those blue eyes.

My pen touched the paper and seemed to take on a life of its own. Words flowed from me and when I set the pen down to read what I had written, I allowed the peace to settle over me.

The roar of the ocean, the quiet of the colorful sky
Quiet meets the roar, blending into peace

Making the Rules

I sit and wonder of our chances of ever capturing the secret
Will peace ever quiet the roar of the world?

The roar of the ocean, the quiet of the colorful sky
I sit in awe, peacefulness embracing me.

I forgot about everything from this weekend, from the past couple of weeks that had weighed me down. I gave myself permission to let go of the hurt and pain, the sadness, the longing, but, most importantly the negative thoughts of self-worth of myself. I closed my eyes and allowed myself the freedom to let my mind flow and wander with no set purpose, no inner reflection and no contemplation of my life. Freedom. What I have wanted all these years.

Then the unthinkable happened. My mind filled with what ifs. What if I hadn't pushed Jack away? What if I had gotten pregnant that day? Jack's child. A lone tear rolled down my cheek. How many times had I wished I had had a part of him with me all these years? What if things had been different? But they weren't. I had made a unilateral decision that had sent us down separate paths, a journey that, apparently, we were destined to take separately.

I pushed the notebook aside. So much for peace. Sunglasses and the smell of salt air was what I needed to clear my head. I grabbed my sunglasses and yanked open the door to find a small box. I glanced around. No one was there. I reached down and picked it up. It was light. I stepped back into the apartment and slipped off my sunglasses. I pulled the ribbon from around the box, and slid open the cover. Inside sat a sand dollar with a note card. I opened the card and read:

*The sand dollar is designed to survive
the storms and represents strength;
yet it's fragile and represents being gentle in your
approach to life. The sand dollar is a reminder to go
with the flow and be flexible in
your way of thinking.*

The card was signed simply, Nick. I picked up the sand dollar and held it in my palm. It was smooth and had been varnished to preserve the hard shell. The intricacies of the pattern on it gave it a unique beauty. I was touched by the meaning behind the sand dollar and the fact that Nick had thought of me when he bought it. Survive storms…well, we certainly have had some life storms lately, and the fragility of our relationship seemed all that clearer now. Flexible in our thinking, I guess that goes two ways. I sighed. It was a clear sign there was some work on being open minded when it came to repairing things with Nick.

I sat there looking at it in my palm. I closed my eyes and envisioned myself free of any walls or barriers that held me back in having a real relationship. Can I leave Jack in the past and, truly, move on? Or was Jack the storm that I had survived and I was now fragile? Was it a metaphor for my relationship with Nick or just for my life? I placed it gently back in the box. Storms of life could come, or even with a relationship. One thing was for sure, I was a survivor.

eleven

Jack

Obligation. The word I had thought about since I had left Charles Winham's office. I did have an obligation to Madde. I had taken vows, and despite our differences, I wasn't going to just walk away. Although, she definitely was making it harder and harder to stay. The plan was to keep my head down and work hard, and then, Charlotte came into our lives. That little girl brightened my day and everything around me.

But the feeling of dread came over me every time I thought about the word obligation. Was it wrong to feel bound to my wedding vows, even if my heart was truly somewhere else? Why did Madde stay if she was so unhappy? And, by her actions, she was extremely unhappy. The sad fact of the matter was that neither of us spoke with the other about what we were really feeling or wanted in life. We both just moved through the days and weeks like nothing had changed in the last two years when, in fact, nothing was truly the same.

Since Izzy had shown up on my doorstep, I had spent so much time reflecting on the past. What could have gone wrong, what could have been if we had stayed together? It was a dangerous path to go down. I had gone down that road while married the first time and it drove a wedge between Michelle and me. Yet, I opened up to Michelle about Izzy and she was the one who kept Izzy between us after that. Though, I don't think I ever had fallen in love with her. Not like I had with Izzy.

The house Neil and I had acquired needed a lot more work than was originally anticipated. Upon closer inspection, the floor boards were found to be rotted. Although the foundation was stable and structurally sound, we decided to level it and start over. I had dropped Charlotte off with my sister and was on my way to meet Neil when, stopped at a red light, I glanced over and saw Madde. She was in a coffee shop sitting alone. I wrestled with the fact of whether I should stop and see if we could talk. Maybe, out of the house and in public, a civil conversation could be had about what each of our expectations were for this marriage, but then I noticed a coat on the chair across from her.

A horn honked behind me indicating the light had turned green and my decision was made for me as I moved forward with traffic towards the house site. I couldn't help but wonder whose coat it was. She didn't mention meeting a friend this morning, and it was in the work day when I would have expected her be at her office. The questions soon fled my mind as I pulled into the driveway of our newly acquired project and saw Neil waiting for me.

The rest of the day was spent walking through the property with our general contractor, making lists and estimating prices for things that needed to be done. Re-

Making the Rules

building would mean a whole brand new house and a high selling price. Neil, on the other hand, usually all about maintaining as much of the original as he could and just renovating, was, for a change, onboard with the new build. It would be knocked flat the next morning and the day after that, we would start the construction.

The day flew by, as was the case with the days when I stayed busy and I pulled into my sister's driveway close to dinnertime. Madde had already texted me and said she would be working late. Questions filled my mind again about who she was with and if she was truly working. Would Madde actually have an affair or did she simply meet a girlfriend to talk out her frustrations with our marriage?

My sister greeted me at the door with Charlotte in her arms. Her dimples deepened when she saw me and held out her arms for me to take her. Any questions in my mind of Madde disappeared as this cherub in my arms eased the negative thoughts from me and filled my heart with joy.

"How was she?" I asked.

My sister shut the door behind me. "Perfect, as always. Staying for dinner?"

"Sure. Madde is working late." My sister glanced at me, but didn't say anything. "We're starting a new project out on Old Route 28."

"New or renovate?" She asked.

"New. Neil wanted to renovate, but there's too much rot and mold inside. New was the only way to go on this one."

My sister moved around the kitchen getting dinner as I sat at the table holding Charlotte. We hadn't spent much time talking about my life lately and I had been debating whether or not tell her about Isabelle showing up. I sighed. Did I risk taking the chance of her being upset? She had not been happy with Isabelle when we broke up, although I know she stayed friendly with her. She had kept me apprised of what Isabelle was doing and I did know that she had moved to Virginia, which was one of the reasons I had been shocked to see her on my doorstep...in New Hampshire.

"Guess who I saw last week."

My sister shook her head at me. "I can't imagine."

I took a deep breath. "Isabelle."

My sister set the spoon down she was holding and turned to look at me. She leaned back against the counter and just watched me for a moment before speaking. "Where did you see her?"

I gave a half smile. "On my doorstep."

"What?" She moved to the table and slid into a chair. "She came to see you? And you're just telling me now?"

"Yes, and yes." I looked down at Charlotte. I didn't want to meet my sister's eyes as I feared she would see how much I still cared for Izzy.

"Jack?" She spoke softly.

I looked up and shook my head. "I don't know why she was there. We didn't get a chance to talk."

"What do you mean?"

"I answered the door and saw her. Before she could say anything this little one spits up all over me. I had to clean up and before I could say anything, she turned and walked away."

"Wait. She came to your house and then turned and left before saying anything to you? That doesn't make sense."

I stood and walked over to the playpen in the corner of the kitchen, placing Charlotte in it with a few toys. Taking a deep breath, I tried to gather my

Making the Rules

thoughts before turning to my sister. "I don't know. She looks good though."

My sister gave me a quizzical look. "Looks good. Jack, what are you saying?"

"Nothing other than she looks good." I gave a small laugh.

"You still care for her." It was a statement. "I know you never stopped loving her. I could see it in your face every time I mentioned something she was doing. It's the reason I stopped telling you things. I didn't want my talking about her to hurt you more."

"It didn't hurt...well, it did, but I wanted to know, too. I always believed there was more to what happened, but she wouldn't talk to me. I still believe her parents played a role in it, but I don't know for sure."

My sister nodded. "I know I never really talked to you about what happened. You never said how the break up happened or what was said, and I didn't want to ask questions because I could see how devastated you were. I probably should have talked with you about it. I waited for Marie to say something whenever I saw her, but she never mentioned it. It was like Isabelle and you had never been together."

"I don't understand that. I felt you had ignored the whole thing, too."

"I never meant for you to feel that way. I thought I was doing you a favor by not talking about it." My sister stood back up to continue with dinner.

"We were young, and hadn't been together very long, but I loved her with everything I had. I wanted to marry her, you know?"

My sister glanced at me. "I didn't know it was that serious between you. It had only been a month or so, right?"

"Five weeks. But it was different than anything I had known to that point or even since. I have never had a relationship where I felt so strongly that it was right, as I did with Izzy."

My sister smiled at the nickname. Very few people had called her Izzy, but I always did and loved that she would light up every time. The memories came back full force...times I had tried not to think about for years. Christmas Eve together and how I had held her in my arms while we talked softly about Christmas. And the memory of our time at the barracks, that memory that was burned into my mind and showed itself often...too often for comfort sometimes. Her innocence and her desire for me shown so clearly, without fear.

"Where'd you go, Jack?" My sister's voice broke through the memories.

"Just thinking of the past." I shrugged. "What's for dinner? Need help?"

My sister knew me too well to know that I wasn't really offering to help with dinner, well, I was and always helped when I could, but she knew it more to be a deflection of the past and talking about Isabelle. She knew how sensitive I was and how much hurt I had suffered after the breakup with Isabelle. Breakup. It was almost comical to call it that. There was no fight, no words of breaking up. It had been Izzy not talking to me and me just walking away, and never talking again. Not much closure for either of us, which is probably why it had hurt so much. Had Isabelle hurt like I had? Did she regret shutting me out? Or was she glad to be rid of me?

"It's ready. Spaghetti with meatballs."

I helped her set the table and brought Charlotte to the table in her high chair, giving her small pieces of a meatball and feeding her some pasta. Peace. This was how life should be, dinner with family.

twelve

Isabelle

I hadn't talked to Nick in a few days, although I had sent him a text thanking him for the sand dollar. Part of me was relieved to have some space to just focus on work and ignore everything else that was falling apart around me, and the other part was wondering why he backed off.

Work had become my haven. I would arrive early morning, most days by six, and didn't leave until close to seven. I was editing the two new authors I had brought on and Gayle had even left the managing of meetings with the marketing and graphic design teams to me. She would sit in on them, but she clearly was allowing me to run point on these two books. Days turned into weeks and I found myself working as the same long hours on the weekend. I had truly become a workaholic and I didn't even seem to notice.

Realizing a month had gone by since that night with Diane and the subsequent fallout with Nick, or really, fallout with Nick and then night at Diane's, I contemplated my life choices one night. For the first time in a month, I packed up my work things at five to head for home. It was Friday and maybe, just maybe, I would only work a half day tomorrow. Diane and I kept in touch daily, but I hadn't had the time to get together with her at all. I did have my next meeting with Mary on Monday since we were only meeting once every six weeks. Had that much time really passed since my return from New Hampshire?

I arrived home and, for once, thought about actually cooking a meal. However, upon further inspection of the fridge, I realized it had been a while since I had done any grocery shopping. I sent Diane a text. Have you eaten yet? Home early for a change.

Within seconds she replied. Flamingo for burgers and drinks?

Meet you there in 20. Dressed in jeans and a t-shirt, I wandered down the boardwalk onto the pier. It was a Friday night, but since the evenings had gotten cooler, the pier wasn't as crowded as it had been in the summer months. September was a great month for the beach. Most kids were back in school and it was mostly just the locals left hanging around. Diane had beat me again when I arrived, but this time, she had found a table off to the side.

"Nice that the tourists are gone." I said as I slid into the chair. "Did you already order?"

"Just margaritas. Wasn't sure you really wanted a burger or if you were going to do your usual salad and make me look bad." Diane grinned.

Making the Rules

The waitress came with our drinks and took our orders. I surprised Diane and ordered a burger with fries. Not my usual meal, but comfort food sometimes was just what was needed.

Once the waitress had left, Diane sat back and looked at me. "Have you seen him?"

"No, but he left a gift outside my door. A sand dollar with this cute little note about how it was a survivor of storms, but fragile, so it needed to be gentle, as approaching life, and to be flexible. It was a cute thought."

Diane smiled. "So, he's trying to make amends, huh?"

I laughed, "Yes, I suppose he is. But the weird thing is, I haven't heard from him at all since. Even when I sent him a thank you text, no response at all."

"But you have been working a lot of hours."

"Yeah, I know. But that has never stopped him before. He used to text throughout the day and stuff."

Diane sipped her drink. "Are you missing that?"

"I don't know, honestly. I'm so busy at work taking on these two new authors that I really don't have time to think about it."

Diane nodded. "And what about other thoughts?"

"Meaning?" I knew what she meant, but needed to stall.

"Jack."

I nodded. "Yes, I think about him. How can I not?"

"I get it, but what are you going to do about it?" Diane asked.

"I don't know. I see Mary Monday. Maybe it's time to talk it out with her."

Diane laughed. "It must be really bad if you think you need to open up in counseling."

"Oh, shut up." Thankfully the food had arrived and I was spared any further ridicule from someone I now considered my best friend.

The evening was spent talking about Diane's love life, or lack thereof, and I spent the evening pointing out potential partners for her.

thirteen

Isabelle

I dragged my feet just a bit getting into Mary's. I knew there were things she was going to immediately dive into, but I was still reluctant to completely open up about the trip.

"How've the past few weeks been?" Mary jumped right into it as soon as the door shut behind me.

"They have been good. I've been busy with work. Long hours the past few weeks. I've taken on two new authors, and Gayle has given me the lead on them."

"And how's Nick?"

I shifted in my chair. "Good, I guess. We had a bit of a blow out and since then he has backed off and hasn't texted me at all. He did leave a gift outside my apartment door, but didn't respond when I thanked him."

"What was the fall-out about?" Mary prodded.

"Him being needy and possessive. He made a snarky comment about having a reunion with Jack. He's hot and cold. First, he's irritable and possessive, and then he's trying to make up for it. He's not the Nick he was before the trip."

"Why do you think that is?"

I stared at her a moment. "I don't know."

"Do you think it's from you leaving on the trip and talking about seeing Jack? Maybe he just needs reassurance as to where you two are in your relationship."

"I don't think so. It's more than that, but I can't put my finger on it. He's jumpy. Honestly, I have been more relaxed without him around, the way he has been."

Mary nodded and waited for me to continue. "You never answered my question last time."

"What question?"

"Did you see Jack?"

"Why is everyone so anxious to find out the answer to that? I told Nick I didn't."

Mary looked at me. "But again, that didn't answer my question."

"I don't want to talk about it yet." My voice was barely a whisper.

"Well, that's a partial answer right there."

I stood and made my way to the window. I looked out at the ocean and just wanted to hear the sounds of the waves. My stomach was churning and anxiety rolled through my chest making it burn.

"Isabelle, come sit, please."

I turned and looked at the chair and then at Mary. I didn't move for a moment and then I made my way back to the chair. "Please, not this subject."

Mary watched me, her eyes boring into me like she could read the beatings of my heart. "When you're ready," she finally said.

I nodded. I tried to slow my breathing as I felt the

Making the Rules

pain in my chest hit me. My breathing accelerated and became shallow. My hand went to my chest as the pain grew.

"Isabelle, deep breaths." Mary was beside me in an instant. "It's a panic attack. Deep breaths, focus on me."

I looked at her and tried to keep my eyes locked with hers. My chest hurt. I closed my eyes and tried to concentrate on my breathing. It seemed like an eternity, but after a half hour passed, the pain subsided and my breathing evened out. Mary was holding my hand.

"Is this the first time you've had a panic attack?"

"Yes. I thought it was a heart attack."

Mary nodded. "Yes, the pain can be pretty intense in the chest area."

"Is this something that is going to happen to me from now on?" I could feel the panic rising again.

Mary squeezed my hand. "No. I think you holding back on some of these topics is what caused it."

Tears filled my eyes.

"What's holding you back, Isabelle?"

"I don't want to feel the pain again. It feels like I just got through feeling like I couldn't handle the guilt of what I did to Jack all those years ago and I just don't want to bring that pain back."

"Was it painful to see him?" Mary asked.

"I didn't tell you I saw him." I deflected.

"You didn't have to. Your body language said it from the first visit we had when you got back." Mary paused. "I didn't push it last time because of the break-in and you talked about your parents, but Isabelle, you have to tell me what happened."

"I went to see him." I stopped and ran the scene through my head again. Driving up his driveway, seeing his yard, his house…wondering if there had been a wife to fix it up, and knocking on his door. The tears that had filled my eyes let go and ran like rivers down my cheeks.

Mary handed me a tissue. "Talk it out."

"I was scared to approach his door, but after the confrontation with my parents and learning about my real mother, I felt invincible…that I could handle anything." I paused. "I wasn't prepared to look into those blue eyes. To see him. I wasn't prepared for the rush of emotions."

"Okay. I take it he opened the door himself so you didn't have to deal with anyone else such as a wife."

I nodded. The tears continued to fall. "He…he…" I cleared my voice.

"He what, Isabelle?"

"I can't." I shook my head and started to stand again.

Mary held up her hand to stop me. "Don't run to the window. We don't have to talk about it, but you can't run from it either."

I sank back into the chair.

"What are you thinking about this whole situation? Forget telling me about seeing him. We'll talk another time about that. But what have your emotions been since you have been back?"

"All over the place. My mind races with what ifs… what if I hadn't pushed him away, what if we had stayed together."

"The what if game is a powerful thing. It can lead you down a dark place if you are not careful. We can't change the past, Isabelle. You can only learn from it and move forward."

I nodded. "I know that. But I wasn't prepared to realize…" I trailed off and stared into space.

"To realize what?" Mary prodded.

"That I still loved him. I gave him my heart all those years ago and he still has it. Does that sound ridiculous?"

Making the Rules

"Quite the contrary. I think it's quite possible that you still love him. There has been no closure."

"How do I get closure?" I asked her.

"That's different for everybody. There is no one definite act that gives you closure. Did you have a conversation at all with him?"

I shook my head. "Not really. He called me by name immediately so, he did recognize me. I left though."

"You left without saying anything."

"It's a long story, but I can't go into it right now."

Mary let it slide, although I knew she wasn't happy about me deflecting again. "Let's stop there tonight. You need to go home and get a good night's sleep. No work tonight. Just rest and let your body recover from the panic attack."

I nodded. "Thank you."

"Let's see each other again in just three weeks instead of waiting so long." Mary suggested.

"Okay." I made the appointment and walked to my car. My thoughts were racing and I couldn't help but feel a tightness in my chest again. I sat in my car and breathed deeply for a while before I felt comfortable enough to drive home. A hot bath and early to bed might just be what I needed and, with any luck, I would sleep through the night.

Fourteen

Jack

As I pulled up in front of Charles Winham's office, I realized that, although I thought I had been dreading this appointment, I actually was looking forward to hearing his insight into this crazy life I had suddenly. The dynamics between Charlotte and Madde had only intensified instead of lessening. Charlotte felt the tension and negative energy that Madde exuded and cried whenever she was around, which just made the negativity from Madde even more present.

Charles was waiting for me when I walked in the door. "Come right in, Jack." I settled into the worn leather arm chair and waited for him to start. The silence continued for a few minutes before he started. "How's Charlotte?"

I immediately relaxed. "She is such a joy. I can't even explain how much that little girl fills my day with happiness."

Charles nodded. "And Madde?"

My smile disappeared. "Nothing new. Charlotte feels

Making the Rules

the tension and cries whenever she is in the room, which of course does not help matters."

"A child can certainly pick up on any ill-will towards them or tension in the air. Have the two of your talked about the situation at all?"

"Not really. One night she wanted to, but Charlotte had been sick and I was exhausted and just couldn't deal with it. When I tried to bring it up in the morning, she refused to talk because she states it was on 'my time table' and not when she wanted to." I shook my head. "I'm so frustrated with the whole situation."

"Let's talk about that. What frustrates you exactly?"

I pondered the question. It was hard to pinpoint exactly what was the launching point of the frustration. "I guess the fact that we can't talk about it, or the fact that she seems to be angry, but won't say what she is angry about."

"And you don't think she's angry that you didn't discuss it with her?"

"Oh, she probably is, but I think there is more to it. When I brought Charlotte home, I truly expected Madde to be thrilled. She had wanted a child so badly. I thought maternal instinct would kick in and she would just love her even if she wasn't her biological child."

"Do you think she wants to, but is holding back because you left her out of the process?"

I stared at him. "I didn't intentionally leave her out. There was no time for a discussion."

"No need to be defensive, Jack. It's a question, not a judgement."

I sighed. "I don't know. There are moments I catch her watching Charlotte and she has almost a pained look on her face. I don't understand what it is about an infant that would hurt her."

"Jack, you know as well as I do that women view things very differently. Do you think it's possible that she's hurting because she couldn't have children?"

"Well, technically she can have a child. It was I who couldn't give her that."

"Right, but she wanted your child...her husband's child. Do you think it could be painful to her that it was something she wanted with you, not for you bring one home to her?"

I ran my hand over my face, trying to erase the irritation. "So, she's mad because she didn't get her own way, instead of being happy that she would still have an opportunity to be a mom." It was a statement and, even as I said it, I could hear the ridiculousness of my tone.

"I think you know that probably isn't the case."

I stood and paced the room. Why had I actually looked forward to this man's insight? It was not really what I wanted to hear, but, then again, when did any of us really want to hear the truth about our faults?

I was pacing the floor in Charles' office. The air hung heavy between us. "Well, Jack?" The question pulled me from my thoughts. I shook my head.

"I don't have an answer. Obligation...it's what makes us stay in situations we don't want to be in. That's the obvious answer, but I'm not sure that's what you are looking for."

"Jack, it's not so much what I'm looking for. You said you stayed in your marriage out of obligation. I asked you to think about what that word means to you." Charles watched me pace and waited.

"To me, obligation is doing the right thing." My mind drifted back to Izzy and my words to her about obligation. No wonder she pushed me away.

"Jack?"

Making the Rules

I shrugged and slid into the chair. "I don't know. Maybe it's my cop-out, my way of not making a decision because I don't know where it will lead me."

"Have you ever had a time where that word has tripped you up, maybe put you on a different path than you wanted to be?"

"Once, I guess. Once, that changed my life forever." I sat back, defeated.

"Okay, well let's start with that."

"There's not much to say. I was in love with a girl eight years ago, made love to her, and then told her there was an obligation there."

"Why was there an obligation? Because you had sex?" Charles had laid his paper and pen aside.

"She was a virgin. I didn't want her to think I had just taken advantage of her, but maybe I did."

"Did you love her?"

I nodded. "Yes." The word was a whisper.

"Did she love you?"

"I…I don't know. She never said, but I never told her either."

"Why did you feel obligated to her, Jack? Lots of girls lose their virginity and they don't have to get married because of it."

I sighed. "I didn't feel obligated to marry her because I was her first. I wanted to marry her because I loved her. I guess I didn't know how to say it and, instead, the word obligation came out and, suddenly, it was over. She pushed me away until I walked away."

Charles just sat there watching me, his expression neutral, not saying a word…just watching. "Do you still love her?"

I met his eyes. "I still care for her very much…is it still love when you haven't seen someone for eight years?"

"It could be. Some people just don't fall out of love over a break-up." Charles leaned forward, his elbows resting on his knees. "The question is that, if you don't still love her, what has stopped you from not living the life you wanted?"

"Haven't I lived the life I wanted? I have a great job, Charlotte is wonderful…" My voice trailed off.

"Yes, your job and your daughter are great things in your life, but you don't have the love of a wife and I'm not sure you have the love for your wife."

Those words hit me hard. No, I certainly didn't love Madde like a husband should love his wife, but I wouldn't say I didn't love her at all. On some level I did still love her. All I had wanted from a marriage was a woman to respect me and love me for who I am. I needed someone in my corner, who would have my back in the tough moments. Someone who, when there were obstacles, would hold my hand and take them head-on with me. "Why does it have to be so complicated?" I asked Charles.

"Is it complicated? Or are you making it complicated because fear has you rooted where you don't want to be?" Charles sat back.

"Of course, it's complicated." I shot back.

"How so?"

"Well," I searched for the right words. "Life is never simple. There are always complications."

"That's not an answer."

I smiled. I knew it wasn't an answer, but more of a deflection because I had no answers. If I had the answers I needed, I wouldn't be sitting here with a therapist. "I don't have the answer, or any answers."

"You don't need all the answers, Jack. You just need to make a move one way or another. Stop being stagnant

Making the Rules

in your life and move forward. Grow from the experiences you have had--with this girl eight years ago, from your first marriage and from your current one. Take those moments that have been tough and realize it's okay that those moments shape your life, just don't let them define your life."

I stared at him. Had I let my experiences shape my life? Even define me? "I'm not sure I understand. Of course, everything we do in life continues to shape us and creates who we are."

Charles nodded. "Yes, but have you allowed yourself to change and grow with these experiences?"

"I'm not sure. How?" I was baffled. I was a smart man; these questions shouldn't be rendering me mute.

"If you continue to live your life feeling obligated to everyone, you aren't changing and growing. You are stuck in a phase of life that leaves you making decisions based on what you feel you have to do, not what you want to do."

"So, you think I should get a divorce?"

Charles shook his head. "That isn't what I said. I think you need to do some soul searching about what is keeping you from moving forward -- either in your marriage or outside of the marriage vows."

I nodded.

"That's your assignment for next time. Think about what it is you want to be doing with your life. What choices would you have made if you hadn't put obligation first?"

I sat in my car after leaving Charles' office and pondered his comments. I had no idea how to even go about thinking about myself, putting myself ahead of anyone. Even when Izzy pushed me away, against my better judgement, I walked away. I had really wanted to pull her into my arms and tell her we could face anything. Instead I did what I knew Izzy wanted, not what was best for us...for me.

Madde. I had no idea where I should even broach things with her. We needed to talk, but I couldn't bring it up, without her balking. But I didn't have a clue how to get her to start the conversation.

fifteen

Isabelle

Tuesday brought the sun and a new perspective on life. I had slept soundly for the first time in months. After the hot bath, and a cup of tea, I had curled up in bed ready to lay there awake and, within minutes, was sound asleep. I was up and dressed in no time, and, yet, I was in no hurry to be at the office at six this morning. Instead of grabbing a travel mug, I poured my coffee into my favorite ceramic mug and took it to the balcony.

Although cool this morning, the sunshine warmed me up sufficiently along with the hot coffee in my hands. As I inhaled the rich aroma before taking that first sip, I was at peace. Maybe Mary was right. I was more anxious about the fact that I refused to talk about Jack than if I did open up about him. I just didn't know how to handle the emotions I was having. Seven years of guilt was one thing, but to let go of the guilt and actually see him, the raw emotions from our time together hitting me again, it was almost too much. I'd rather have the guilt than know how much I still loved him.

I finished my coffee and watched the ocean for a few minutes. With a glance at my watch, I was surprised that it was close to seven already. Just as I finished rinsing my cup and picking up my laptop bag, my phone started ringing. Nick. I was surprised that he was calling this early in the morning, at all really.

"Hello?"

"Hi, Izzy. Already at work?"

"You won't believe it, but no. I actually enjoyed my coffee this morning on the balcony instead of running into work. I'm just headed out the door now."

"Who are you?" Nick laughed.

"I know, right? What's going on with you?" I locked up the apartment and headed to the car while listening.

"I just thought I'd call and see if you had plans for dinner, a late dinner if need be."

He sounded so formal, I couldn't help but smile. "I think I can make sure I'm out of work by six if you want to do dinner."

"Great. Pick you up at 6:30?"

"Sounds good. I'll see you then."

We said our brief good byes and I pondered his call on my drive to the office. It was out of character for him, but he sounded so sincere. Maybe he was making an effort to get back to the old Nick. I needed to make that effort, too. Sand dollar. I reflected on the note card that had been with it. Go with the flow and be flexible in your thinking.

I spent the rest of my day just as productive as if I had been there at six and by five-thirty, I was wrapping up things and ready to head home. By the time Nick

Making the Rules

knocked at the door, I had changed into a more casual skirt and blouse with a pair of flats.

I opened the door and found Nick holding a single pink rose. I smiled and gestured for him to come in.

"You look beautiful." He handed the rose to me.

"Thank you. You clean up pretty well yourself. Let me just put this in water."

Nick waited in the living room while I went to the kitchen. I smiled. It was so reminiscent of a first date that I couldn't help but wonder if he was nervous. When I returned to the living room, Nick was waiting patiently by the door.

"Ready?" I picked up my clutch and had my keys ready to lock the door.

"When you are." Nick responded.

The air was cool outside, but with my long-sleeved blouse, I was comfortable. The smell of the salt air was strong tonight and I inhaled deeply. "I reserved us a table at "The Chef's Table"."

"Great. I've been dying to try that place, but it's always mobbed."

Nick nodded. "We were lucky. Apparently, there weren't many tables left. They usually only take reservations and no walk-ins because they are so full."

Small talk continued as we drove the short distance to the restaurant. I talked about work and the new authors I was working with, the excitement and stress of taking on the lead of these two new books. I felt like I was rambling, but Nick just listened and nodded appropriately to encourage me to keep talking.

The restaurant was aglow with bright lights inside seeping through the tinted windows, and small twinkling lights hung around outside along the roof edge and door frame.

"Am I underdressed?" I turned to Nick as we approached the door.

"Not at all. You look great." He smiled and reached for my hand. He placed it in the crook of his elbow, giving it a little squeeze as we walked in the restaurant.

"The Chef's Table" inside was every bit the image of intimacy and romance. Lights were low, with candles on each table. Soft music was piped in through speakers, not elevator music either, just soft romantic music that one could dance to. There was a dance floor over on the edge of the main floor. We followed the hostess as she led us as a few steps to a section that gave the impression of an alcove with only a handful of tables for two.

I couldn't help but look around to try and take it all in. "This is beautiful, Nick. I never imagined it would look like this inside."

"Yeah, it's pretty amazing."

"Have you been here before?" I hadn't even opened the menu yet, and was still glancing around to take in different aspects of the room.

"No, only in the door to make the reservation." Nick answered.

I glanced over to him to find him watching me. "I must look like a silly teenager gawking at everything."

He grinned. "Not at all, but I don't think I have seen you this enthralled in anything besides your work. It's nice to see you appreciate something else."

It felt like a blow, although I'm not sure he meant it that way. "I suppose I do get a bit caught up in work. The hazard of loving your job, I guess."

Nick reached for my hand. "There is nothing wrong with that, Izzy. I didn't mean to imply otherwise."

Making the Rules

I nodded and held his hand. "I know I get self-absorbed sometimes, Nick. And I'm sure it's irritating to those around me."

Nick squeezed my hand. "I don't recall us ever really fighting about you working too much. Usually our disagreements come from anything getting too personal or intimate."

I knew he was right, but it hurt just the same to hear the words. I sounded like such a bitch, but I know I've kept him at arm's length and even the girls in my life, I've never let close. Diane is the one exception to that rule. For some reason, she and I are kindred souls. We have both shared some difficulties growing up and through our young adult lives, so far. Although I didn't know the details from her difficulties, she had shared enough that I knew she carried some guilt as I have from some life choices.

"So, what's good here? Have you heard any recommendations?" I pulled my hand back so I could open the menu. It was a small menu, which, in my opinion, was a plus. I hated too many choices.

The waitress approached and told us the specials. I opted for the roasted chicken dinner. She poured us a glass of wine from the bottle Nick had ordered ahead of time. It was a rich red wine, and although I don't usually drink red wines, I found it was smooth without the typical bitter after taste.

We sat in silence as I continued to look around, trying to be discrete. The intricate carvings in the post and beams were of flowers. The more I looked at it, the more different types I found that had been carved to look like they were on a vine that continued around the room. And what a variety it was.

I finally looked back at Nick and found him watching me with an amused smile on his face. "Okay, go ahead and say it."

"Say what?"

"I'm not sure what you're thinking, but I get the impression that you are finding me quite funny tonight with my gawking at everything."

Nick laughed. "Not really funny, but you do look like you don't get out much."

My face flushed and I cast my eyes down to the table.

"You are so beautiful when you blush, Izzy. I have missed you."

I brought my eyes up to meet his. "I've missed you, too. I was surprised when you didn't even answer when I texted you about the sand dollar. That was amazing, by the way. The way they explained the meaning in the card…I really liked that."

"I was just trying to give you some space. I figured we both needed to step back and process things that have happened. I am sorry about that last night, in your room. I never meant to make you feel like I was pressuring you."

"I know. And I probably overreacted a bit. It has taken me a bit to process on my own, and with Mary's help, the confrontation with my parents."

"Do you want to talk about it?" Nick asked. There was no hint of demand, just a simple question.

"Maybe some time, but not tonight. Let's just enjoy tonight without any depressing talk." I sat back as our food arrived and we were silent as we started eating. By the end of the evening, Nick and I were laughing and at ease with each other again. The familiar teasing was back and it felt like I had never left for New Hampshire.

We drove back to my place in silence. I could only

Making the Rules

imagine where his thoughts were, but mine were rehashing the evening and the enjoyment I had felt. I wanted, for the first time in quite a while, for Nick to stay with me tonight. But true to myself, I wasn't about to ask. Let's face it, I was never going to be that woman.

"Feel like a little walk on the beach before going inside?" Nick asked as he parked the car.

"Always." There was nothing like listening to the waves with the moon shining off the water. The moonlight caused little sparkles in the water, almost like diamonds, throughout the ocean. For me, there was nothing more peaceful.

We walked hand in hand to the rocky section and then headed back. I would have loved to climb up to our spot in the rocks, but neither of us was dressed for it. "What is it about being near the ocean at night that is just so peaceful?" I wondered out loud.

"It is peaceful, isn't it? It's always been a favorite place of mine."

I glanced at him. "Have you always lived near the ocean? You never spoke about where you grew up."

"We moved around a lot when I was a kid. I don't think there is one place that I really call home."

I nodded. "That must have been tough as a child."

"Sometimes. But other times, it was nice, especially if we were moving from a place that I didn't seem to fit into."

"You not fit in? Something tells me you could charm anyone, no matter where you were." Tonight, the flirting was easy.

"I wasn't always such a charmer." Nick's voice was low and I had the impression that he was becoming melancholy with reflection.

"Well, we definitely change as we get older. I like to think, for the better." I responded.

"That is so true." Nick grinned at me.

Nick stopped when we arrived at my door. "Aren't you coming in?"

"I don't think so, not tonight."

I looked at him puzzled. "Why not?"

"Izzy, it was a great night. Let's just go back to taking it slow." He pulled me close. His lips soft and gentle on mine, his tongue teasing me before he broke off the kiss and stepped back. "Have a good night. Thank you for tonight."

He waited while I opened the door and stepped in. I glanced back at him. He gave me a reassuring smile before he turned to leave.

I closed the door and locked up. Leaning against the door, I tried to figure out what just happened. It was nice, very chivalrous, that he didn't come in, but damn it, it's not like we are just starting to date. Sex was not usually something he shied away from. I had mixed emotions about where this was headed and confused by Nick's use of taking it slow.

sixteen

Isabelle

As the three weeks passed, and my next appointment with Mary drew closer, the anxiety in me increased. Although there had been no further panic attack, I was on edge constantly. I knew the time was coming where I would have to talk about Jack and she wouldn't let it slide anymore. She had been patient with me, but I also knew that, if she didn't push the issue, I wasn't going to talk about it.

Monday evening approached after a long day of meetings. I had an alarm set for the time I would need to leave to get to Mary's office and, being engrossed in emails, I startled when it went off. I groaned inwardly and started packing up.

"Isabelle, do you have a minute?" Gayle called from her office.

I walked to the doorframe. "I have an appointment I have to get to, but I can spare a couple of minutes."

"No worries. Let's meet tomorrow. I just want an update from you regarding where you are in the edits for these two new books. I have some earlier time slots for releases and didn't know if you would be able to make it work to, at least, have one of them fill a slot."

"How much sooner are we talking?" I asked.

"I'd like one of them to be moved up from May to February."

I nodded. "Let me take a look tonight to see where the final round of edits is and how soon I think they will be back. I think, probably, one of them won't have a problem with a shortened deadline. I'll let you know tomorrow."

"Perfect. See you tomorrow."

I had gotten used to Gayle's abrupt dismissals and, now, could laugh about it. But, when I had first started working for her, I took it way too personal and used to go home imagining the worst things. Over the past year, working with her, I have found that she is more abrupt with the people she trusts. It has become a comforting feeling to be dismissed in such a manner now.

Glancing at my watch, I saw that I would be a few minutes late if I didn't hustle. Thankfully, there wasn't much traffic and I made it to Mary's in record time. I walked in the door just as the bell chimed six.

Mary closed the door behind me and waited for me to settle into a chair. "Any more panic attacks?"

"None. Thank God."

"Good." She paused, but when I didn't speak she continued. "What's new since we last talked?"

"Nick took me out on a date. Seemed odd since it's

Making the Rules

not something that we, really, have ever done. We usually just meet somewhere. This was like a real thing, he picked me up and had made reservations. We walked on the beach before he walked me to my apartment."

"Walked you to your apartment?" Mary looked at me.

"Yeah. He wouldn't come in. In fact, he has refused to stay at my place at all. Says he wants to 'take it slow'."

"And how do you feel about that?"

I snickered. "Love the way you phrase your questions." I shrugged. "At first it seemed odd, but I guess it really doesn't bother me. Maybe it's a bit nice."

"It doesn't bother you because, maybe, you don't want him there?"

I shook my head. "I don't think that's it. It just seems different. Maybe I've never been…I don't even know what to call what we are doing. Dating?"

"Sounds like he's courting you."

I was puzzled. "Courting…like old fashion courting?"
Mary nodded.

"I'm not sure I care for that phrase. It makes me feel like the end result is marriage."

"You don't want to be married?" Mary asked.

"I don't know. Maybe someday, but it's not high on my list, right now, of things I want to do."

"What is high on your list?"

I shrugged. "Work. I'd like to travel some before I settle down."

"You could travel with a spouse."

"Yeah, but it's not the same."

Mary put her pad of paper and pen aside. "Not the same, or not Jack?"

Here we go. She finally got around to bringing up Jack. I was foolish to think that we could keep the whole session on Nick and me without any mention of Jack. "It's not about Jack."

"I think everything you do, whether consciously or subconsciously, has Jack in the undertones."

"That's not true." I tried to be indignant, but part of me felt she may be right.

"Are we going to talk about seeing Jack on your trip?" Mary finally asked the direct question I had been avoiding.

"I don't know if I'm ready." I started and trailed off.

Mary shook her head. "Try again."

"Why do you push me on this?" I stood and walked to the window.

"Because, if I don't, you will push all the emotions down and we both know that does more harm than good. You have to talk about this, Isabelle."

I knew she was right, but I wasn't ready. Or I just didn't want to. I wanted the memory of seeing him to stay with me, without analyzing it. Mary was silent behind me, waiting. I could feel her eyes on me. I slowly turned to face her, but stayed by the window. Distance was good.

"Yes, I saw him. He opened the door and there he stood. I looked into those blue eyes and it was like time hadn't passed at all." I paused.

"You said he recognized you?" Mary asked.

"Yes. He immediately said 'Izzy' and I just nodded. I couldn't stop looking at him. He stood there, holding a baby. A baby." I walked toward the chair as my legs felt like they would buckle. "He looked so good and at ease holding the baby. I couldn't help but think, what if that had been our child?" Tears filled my eyes, which seemed a common occurrence these days at Mary's office.

"A baby." Mary watched me. "That's a pretty permanent fixture in someone's life."

Making the Rules

I nodded, unable to speak.

"Isabelle, what happened? You didn't say anything?"

As I sat there recalling the moment, I could see Jack opening the door, the baby on his shoulder as he rubbed it's back. The look of confusion on his face as he realized who I was and both of us just looking at each other. I had wanted to speak.

"There wasn't time really." I started laughing. "As luck would have it, the baby took that moment to spit up on him, all over his shoulder and running down his back. His only words were 'I have to tend to this'. I don't know if he intended to talk with me after or not, I just nodded, turned, and walked away."

Mary stared at me. "That was it?"

I nodded. "That was it."

"That's not closure, Isabelle."

"I know. It's one of the reasons it's been so hard. I wanted to apologize to him, to, hopefully, be able to talk out what happened, but then there was nothing. No words between us, nothing. I have no idea what he was thinking and I can't get the sight of him holding a baby out of my mind."

It seemed unbearable to think about, but the sight of Jack with a child…what woman's heart doesn't melt when she sees the man she loves holding a baby? I glanced at Mary. "Seeing him like that, I realized I had never stopped loving him. And I don't know how to handle that." There. I had said it. I was admitting defeat.

"No one would, Isabelle. This isn't the end of the world, you just have to work through the emotions and, after you get through that, then see where you are. Sometimes just processing the information can make a world of difference."

"And I lied to Nick about seeing him. He seemed so jealous, I couldn't tell him what happened."

Mary nodded. "I figured that part out already. And maybe, for now, it's for the best that he doesn't know. At least until after you can process it yourself."

We spent the remainder of the hour talking about strategies to help me think it through. Even so, by the time we finished talking, I was no closer to knowing how to deal with this than I had been before. But, it was out in the open now with Mary, and Diane knew, so the burden wasn't so great for me to bear alone.

seventeen

Jack

I was late getting home. I never could pick up Charlotte from my sister's house and get out of there quickly. I know she meant well, but my sister was pushing for me to forget about Isabelle. Finally, not being able to take it anymore, I broke down and told her about going to counselling and how Izzy was a big part of my thoughts right now, not so much because how I was feeling about her, but because there were so many uncertainties in my life that I had no idea what to do about. I admitted to her that I had no plan of action for what direction I wanted my life to go.

When I finally drove up to my house, it was dark. Madde's car was nowhere to be seen. She hadn't said she was working late, and a small niggling in the back of my mind brought to the forefront the coat on the chair across from her at the coffee shop. I shook the thought away.

There was no way Madde would do that to me. She may be mad at me, but she wouldn't throw away our marriage vows…would she? Was it possible that I was the only one who felt a sense of obligation to our wedding vows?

After bathing Charlotte and reading her a bedtime story, I had settled her down and was sitting quietly in the living room when Madde walked in the door. She stopped short when she saw me just sitting there. "Everything okay?" She asked.

"Shouldn't it be?" I replied.

She shrugged, but didn't speak.

"Where have you been?" The question was quiet and held no accusation, but sounded so defeated, even to my own ears.

She turned to look at me. "Out, why?"

"Since when, if you are 'out', do you not bother to say you won't be home for dinner? Have we lost any common courtesy between us?"

She seemed to search my face for signs of what…anger, sadness? She didn't answer for a moment and then she walked over and sat on the couch. "Maybe we can finally have a conversation, if that is alright with you." The snarkiness of her words immediately put me on edge, yet this is the conversation I wanted.

"Sure." I waited for her to speak.

She cleared her throat. "This is ridiculous, Jack. Neither one of us is happy."

"Is it because of Charlotte? I don't understand you being so hateful to her." She started to speak, but I raised my hand to stop her. "Yes, I understand you being mad at me because I didn't talk to you before I brought her home, but there truly was no time."

"I wouldn't have brought her home like a stray cat.

Making the Rules

The mother had other options." Her words were like a glass of ice water hitting me in the face. Could she really be that heartless?

"Madde."

"Don't Madde me. It's my turn now. Just listen for a change." She took a deep breath. "We haven't been on the same page for a long time, Jack...long before you brought her home."

I broke in. "Her? Charlotte is her name."

She just shook her head at me. "I don't really care, Jack, how attached you are to her. Great, good for you. I'm not attached to her, I will never be attached to her and I don't want anything to do with raising her. This was your opportunity to have a child that you couldn't have. I can have my own child. I don't need someone else's to raise to complete me."

I was stunned. "You think I took in Charlotte just because I thought she was my only chance for a child? I wanted to adopt, you never did." I ran my hand over my face, trying to shake the feeling of dread that was over-coming me.

"Wasn't she? This was a unilateral decision that you made."

Unilateral. The same word I had used about Izzy all those years ago. She made the decision to push me away and I had allowed her, and it had killed me. Was I un-intentionally doing the same thing, still angry that Izzy hadn't allowed me in on the decision making? Did I do that to Madde?

"I'm sorry, Madde." I sighed. "I truly am. I never meant for this to become a wedge between us."

The anger was gone from her as she looked at me. "I know. I know you didn't do it intentionally, but you did do it and I don't think there is any coming back from this."

"What are you saying?"

She stood and looked down at me. "I think we need to each think about our options and how we want to move forward. This…" she gestured between us, "hasn't been good for a long time."

Before I could respond, she had left the room and I heard the bedroom door click softly. The anger was gone from the house, but instead a sadness permeated the air. And the crux of the matter was, I knew exactly what option I wanted. The real question was, how did I move forward and find a new me…the me who has been dying to be set free for years.

The next few days I stayed busy with our newest house project. I was comfortable leaving Charlotte with family and she loved going to my sister's. The only areas of my life that seemed easy were my role in Charlotte's life and my job. Everything else was a mess. Madde and I hadn't really talked since that night. We went through our days living as roommates more than anything. We no longer ate meals together or knew each other's schedules. Honestly, I suddenly was more at ease in my own house than I had been in years.

I had another week before I went back to see Charles and I had been trying to find a way to grow from these experiences. The truth of the matter was, I had gotten nowhere. My mind always went back to "I did what I needed to do, the right thing", but it was never what I had wanted to do. Right from the moment Izzy pushed me away, I had done what she wanted me to do -- walk away and, for whatever reason, keep walking. I had done it, but I had never felt right about it. I had wallowed in

Making the Rules

guilt over that fateful night. Relived every moment of that day in my barracks, trying to find a clue that she had told me she didn't want it...but, in reality, when I pulled back, she asked me not to stop. I knew in my heart that I hadn't forced her to do anything, but, what was I missing from that day?

What did I do wrong to make her push me away? In my mind, the word 'obligation' was a contributing factor, but in my gut, I had always felt that her parents were behind it. Had they forced her to break up with me? I'd never had the impression that they really liked me and they definitely didn't like the fact that we were dating. I had believed that the only reason they had allowed it was because they knew my sister through church.

This thought process had become circular. No answers, but a never-ending circle of questions. I tried the list approach. Pros and Cons of all my experiences from Izzy, to my first marriage, to Madde and me. The only con with Izzy was walking away. My first marriage...well that had been a disaster right from the start with me marrying her for the wrong reasons and then there was Madde. I had truly thought I loved her when we married, but two years into it, I felt that it, too, was nothing more than me trying to do the right thing. Had she ever loved me? I thought so, at the beginning, but as soon as she found out I couldn't have children, the distance between us grew. Where did the list leave me? Nowhere. How could I grow from these life experiences, if I had no idea what they were teaching me? I sighed. I had to be overthinking it, but I had no idea how to go about it in a different way.

I had left the job site and was headed back home and, stopping at the same red light, I glanced over, again, to the same coffee shop where I had seen Madde previously.

There she was again, sitting at the same table, alone. I made a hasty decision and pulled over to find a parking space. I jogged across the street to the coffee shop and entered just as Madde stood with a smile on her face. A feeling of relief washed over me that she was happy to see me, until a man walked in front of me and pulled her into his arms. Shock paralyzed me to the spot until I heard a "wanna move out of the doorway?" I moved to the side as two young girls pushed by me, sending me a glare. I mumbled an apology and turned and walked out the door.

Madde hadn't seen me and that probably was a good thing. I stood on the sidewalk for a minute debating whether to ignore what I had seen, or to go back inside and confront them. I wasn't one for confrontation, but I was livid. Two years. Just two years we had been married and she couldn't even get out of the marriage before she jumped into another man's arms. The anger ate at me as I crossed the street to my vehicle, and continued as I drove home.

Obligation was gone from my vocabulary as I drove home. My anger grew to just about a boiling point as I was driving up the driveway. The sense of doing the 'right thing' was gone. All I wanted was her gone. I hadn't gone to pick up Charlotte. Instead I had texted my sister and let her know I would be late, but I would explain when I got there.

I opened the garage and located some old boxes that were broken down from the move to the house just a little over a year ago. Finding the packing tape, I put the boxes together and started filling them. Madde's clothes, jewelry, shoes, pictures she had bought. The furniture was staying and if she wanted to fight for it, she would have a fight. By the time I was done, there was not a speck

Making the Rules

of Madde's touch anywhere to be seen. I taped up the boxes and put them outside the garage door on the tar of the driveway. I stood there for a moment contemplating whether or not I had time to run to the hardware store to get new locks, and if I should reprogram the code for the garage door opener. I knew, legally, I couldn't do it, but anger was still pulling the strings within me.

I was standing inside the garage at the key pad still debating over changing the code when Madde drove in. She stopped in front of the boxes, seeing they were blocking her way to drive into the garage. As she exited the car, she saw me. "What's this?"

I turned to her and walked a few steps closer to her. "Your stuff."

"What? You packed up my stuff? Are you kicking me out?" There didn't seem to be anger on her part, just shock and disbelief.

"Maybe you would like to call your boyfriend to come help you pick them up." I just stared at her as my words registered and her eyes widened.

"What, how?" She couldn't seem to find any words.

"I saw you at the coffee shop, alone actually, and was going to come in and see if we could talk about our conversation the other night. Just as I walked through the door, imagine my surprise to see another man holding you." I shrugged. "I take it that's your decision...the option you have chosen."

"Jack. I never meant to hurt you."

"Are you kidding me right now? Never meant to hurt me? You sit there and play the victim because of Charlotte, but, in the meantime, you are screwing around behind my back?" My anger imploded once again. "How long has it been going on?"

"Jack, does it matter?" Madde pleaded with me.

"Yes, it does. How long?"

She sighed as she opened her back door and went to pick up the first box. "About a year."

"A year!" This was not what I had expected. I had thought she had pulled this stunt because of Charlotte. "A year, long before Charlotte was even in our lives you were screwing around…a year after our wedding."

She nodded. "Jack, it's not like either of us was happy."

"Don't even try to justify that. I don't want you anywhere near this house again. I'll go to the lawyer tomorrow and have divorce papers drawn up and will have the lawyer send them to your office."

She finished putting the boxes in her car. "Is there nothing left of mine in the house?"

"Nothing. Everything you came into the marriage with, or have bought since we were married, is in those boxes."

She played with her keys for a moment before tossing me her house key. "Don't worry, Jack. I won't be back. I'll sign the papers as soon as I get them. I want nothing from you." She turned and got back into her car. I just stood there and watched as she drove down the driveway. I looked down at my hand and the key that she had given me.

There was no doubt in my mind now, the code on the garage door opener would be changed tonight and the door locks tomorrow on the house. The anger that had fueled the past couple of hours dissipated and I realized I was relieved. The decision was made, she had made it for me and I didn't even care.

eighteen

Isabelle

As September turned to October and the weather cooled considerably, I had one of my new authors push up their release date so the work had doubled, it seemed overnight. The other author wasn't ready to move things up, but Gayle seemed happy that one had. I was working, pretty much, around the clock to get things ready for the release date, which, although five months away, was still overwhelming to get everything done.

Nick and I had fallen into a comfortable routine of going out a few times a week and back to texting almost daily. However, he still refused to stay overnight and I was getting irritated by the whole situation. It was just sex. When did he grow such a conscience? I had put Jack from my mind, or I had tried to. I would find myself searching social media for glimpses of him and his family, but his pictures were typically of him alone. I had no idea what his life was like--was he married, was that his child? If I wasn't careful, I could easily get caught up in the past.

I spent some of my free time working on new poems and found a peace when I could put something to paper. It seemed to even out my emotions, for the most part, and I was able to write about Jack and my feelings regarding him, love lost, and missed opportunities.

I found myself in the middle of October on a Saturday with no motivation to work from home. I poured myself coffee in my travel mug, bundled up in an oversized hoodie and started for the rocks, a spot of self-reflection. I arrived to find the spot sunny and, at least when I was sitting, fairly sheltered from the wind off the ocean. I sipped my coffee and watched the waves crash on the rocks. Mesmerized by the sound and the motion, I didn't hear Nick approaching. I startled when he slid onto the rock next to me.

"Hey. It's been a while since we were here together."

"Quite a while. What are you up to today?" I snuggled a little closer to him.

"Not much. Thought I'd just relax here with my coffee. At least, seeing you this time, I didn't spill it."

I smiled as I remembered our first encounter and how he had dropped his coffee in surprise at me being in 'his' spot. "Yes, you weren't all that pleasant without your coffee."

"Please. I was the utmost gentleman considering you hijacked my spot."

I snorted. "Hijacked your spot. You were invading my space."

He intertwined his fingers with mine without another word. It was the first time in a long time that things

Making the Rules

felt absolutely back to the beginning. I leaned my head on his shoulder and continued to watch the waves. Neither of us spoke, but just enjoyed the moment. A rarity these days for both of us, it seemed. The Nick who had been on edge through the month of September seemed to have relaxed and found his inner peace again.

"Can I ask you something?" I ventured.

"Of course."

"What was going on with you last month? You seem different now. It was like you were so on edge in September."

"I hadn't noticed." It seemed like a vague answer and a deflection, which I recognized since it is my signature move.

"Okay." I wanted to push further, but he had dismissed the question and I didn't want to ruin the moment we had.

"I'm sorry if you felt that way, Izzy. September sometimes is a hard month for me. I lost someone I loved dearly in September and, around the anniversary of the death, I guess I get a little lost, for lack of a better word."

"I understand and that makes sense. I'm sorry for your loss." I wanted to ask who it was, but something about his demeanor told me the subject was closed. As much as I hated to admit it, it was a bit of a comfort knowing that he wouldn't share everything with me. It almost gave me permission to be okay with not telling him everything. It wasn't like we were keeping secrets from each other, but I also felt we weren't at a place where we had to share everything.

Did we have a sort of a relationship, undefinable in my mind? Sure. But I never considered it serious enough to bare my soul to him. Apparently, he didn't either, as much as he would like to give the impression that I was the only one who was closed off. In reality, we both were closed off in some sections of our lives. Maybe we aren't made to share everything with the ones we care about, especially if it could be hurtful to them. In my nonsensical logic, I could bring it all around to keeping things from someone is more about protecting them. Isn't that what I had done with Jack? Protected him from the shameful person who had tried to kill herself?

"You working today?" Nick's voice broke through my thoughts.

"Part of me thinks I need to, but the other part is tired of work. I feel like it has been relentless, around the clock lately, getting ready for the book release and, maybe, I just need, at least, a few hours of not thinking of work."

Nick nodded. "If you are thinking that, you probably are way overdue for some down time."

"Probably." I agreed. "How about another cup of coffee? I can brew up a fresh pot."

Nick agreed and stood, pulling me up with him. "Sounds good."

We had no sooner entered the apartment when my cell phone rang. I looked at the caller ID and saw Officer Terrell's name and number. "I have to take this."

"Of course."

I took the phone to the kitchen. "Hello?" I answered while preparing the coffee to brew.

"Ms. LaFayette?"

"Yes."

"This is Officer Terrell and I just wanted to let you know we are still working on your break-in. We had a

Making the Rules

lead come in that there may have been a witness who saw someone coming out of your apartment."

"Well, that's good news. When will you know more?"

"I'm headed to meet with them now. I will keep you posted. I just wanted to check to make sure you haven't had any other issues."

"None at all. Thank you for the recommendation of the dead bolt. If nothing else, it's an added feeling of security."

"No problem at all. I'll let you know when we have more information."

"Thank you." I hung up the phone just as the coffee had finished.

"Who was that?" Nick spoke behind me.

"That was the police officer who came here when my apartment was broken into."

"Oh?" Nick's voice was questioning, but there was something about the tone that make me turn to look at him.

"They think they have a witness who saw someone coming out of my apartment. They are going to talk with the person today."

Nick crossed the kitchen and filled his coffee mug, and then mine. "Do you really think, after all this time, a witness has come forward? Or that it would even be accurate?"

"I don't know, but I hope so. It would nice to have this tied up and know that they caught this jerk who trashed my place."

Nick gave me a puzzled look. "I thought you said nothing was taken?"

"Nothing was, but I've had to replace all my kitchen dishes and glasses as well as the picture frames in the living room. The place was a mess. Whether they took anything or not, they violated my space."

He nodded before heading to the living room. I stared after him wondering what I said that changed his attitude. He had gone from the old Nick back to the Nick of September, irritable and grouchy. I shook my head. Deep breath. Hopefully, it was just out of concern for me that the topic seemed to irritate him. In the back of my mind, though, there was this niggling feeling that something was going on.

By the time, I walked into the living room, the dark cloud over Nick seemed to dissipate and he was back to the man I knew. Silence filled the room as neither of us seemed to know what to say. "Nick?"

"Yeah."

"What's going on?"

"What do you mean?"

"You just seemed to get distant after the phone call from the police department."

Nick shrugged. "Brings back some memories, I guess."

"Of what?"

Nick looked at me. "I told you I lost someone dear to me in September, a few years ago."

"Yes."

"It was a break-in gone wrong. I guess that's why I got so upset that you didn't call me when your apartment was broken into."

"I had no idea. I'm sorry, Nick."

He pulled me closer to him on the couch. "It's okay. You had no way of knowing. I guess the phone call just made me think that you might not be totally safe here by yourself."

Making the Rules

"I think I'm safe. I have the dead bolt now and there hasn't been anything since I got back to indicate someone is still targeting me. I think Officer Terrell was right that someone just knew I wasn't here so it was an easy target."

"Maybe."

I looked up at him and smiled. "You have been asked to stay, but you have refused."

"I wanted to take it slow. To give you the time and space I thought you needed."

"I understand that. But don't play the protector when it was you who refused to stay." I was teasing, but the look that crossed Nick's face was rage before it disappeared and he smiled.

"Aren't you the one who says you don't need protecting?" He countered.

"Absolutely. I can take care of myself." I was joking to a point, but I also didn't want him to think I was helpless. Helpless was never a word I would use to describe me. Pig-headed and stubborn, maybe, helpless, no.

Nick shook his head. "You're impossible."

I grinned at him and snuggled in close.

"What if we went away one weekend? Just you and me, act like tourists and leave work behind."

I sat up and looked at Nick. "When and where?"

"You'd consider it?"

I smiled. "Yes, depending on when and where."

"How about the end of October, the last weekend. We can just go somewhere on the coast, not that far, drivable."

I nodded. "Did you have some place in mind?"

Nick's eyes shone like a child's on Christmas morning. "I've heard the end of October is the sea turtle hatching time. Emerald Isle in North Carolina is supposed to be well known for this. We could go and see if we see the turtle hatching and their race for the ocean."

"That would be cool. Little tiny turtles hatching. I have heard it's an amazing thing to witness. I would love that."

"Good. I'll make the arrangements. I think it's like a two and half to three-hour drive. We could leave after work, or early Saturday morning."

"I could probably arrange to be out of work by around four or a little after and we could leave then. That would give us two nights." My heart fluttered a bit. A weekend away with Nick. It could be just the thing to get me past the hump of holding him at arm's length, and to forget Jack. I closed my eyes for a moment. I can't even think about a weekend away with Nick without Jack's name popping into my mind.

nineteen

Jack

I arrived at my sister's just in time to eat dinner with her. Charlotte broke into a huge grin as soon as I walked in and any apprehension I had been feeling about the day was washed away. It was the right thing that had been done and it couldn't have waited. I felt no guilt at packing up Madde's stuff and throwing her out of the house. In fact, it felt good to have acted on the situation and I did what needed to be done.

I immediately started setting the table and talked with Charlotte as she sat in her high chair. She babbled back, brightening my day even further. It wasn't until we had sat down and our plates had food on them that my sister cleared her throat.

"Well?"

I glanced at her. "Madde moved out today."

"She moved out?"

I smiled. "Yes, with a little help from me. Technically, a lot of help from me. Her stuff was boxed and in the driveway waiting for her when she arrived."

"Oh, no. What happened?" My sister's lips curled just a little and I recognized her trying hard to keep from smiling.

"I saw her at the coffee shop with another man. She now tells me it has been going on for a year. So much for being so hurt about me bringing Charlotte home." I shrugged.

"Wow." She studied me. "Good for you. I think you did the right thing."

I turned my attention to Charlotte and fed her a spoonful of squash. "Honestly, I feel so relieved. At first I was angry, but now...just relieved."

After returning home with Charlotte and putting her to bed, I found myself wandering around the house enjoying having thoughts of how I could redecorate it and make it my own. When we had bought the house, Madde had been insistent that a man didn't have a decorating bone in his body and decided to do all the interior decorating. I had let her, just to keep the peace. Another example of how I despised confrontation and would avoid it at all costs.

I grabbed a beer from the fridge and sank onto the couch. I flipped onto the sports channel and put on a hockey game. The insanity of what just happened finally hit me as I sat there with the TV on, looking around the living room. What had I done? Did I just act in a fit of emotions or was I finally rational?

The next morning, a peacefulness filled the house as Charlotte made a mess with her breakfast. I sipped my coffee as I watched her play with her Cheerios. She seemed to sense the change in the house and was all smiles. I had been raising this sweet girl by myself, in essence, since I

Making the Rules

brought her home, but it suddenly hit me that I was truly alone--a single parent.

My mind filled with the awareness and the mental list-making started: household, work, babysitter for Charlotte. I wanted to become more involved at the job site and the flipping of the houses, and this would just be part of the new lifestyle we were going to have. The weight on my shoulders was lifted. I grabbed a pad of paper and started writing out what needed to be sorted. What hours would I work? Who would watch Charlotte while I was working? I needed to keep her schedule fairly similar to make both of our lives easier.

First things first, find a divorce lawyer. This charade of a marriage was over. Packing up Madde's things the day before had been therapeutic and broken through the innate feeling of obligation. I started fumbling through the yellow pages while Charlotte finished up her breakfast. I inhaled deeply. I never dreamt I would be going through a second divorce. It grated on me that my life had been changed so drastically from what I had pictured when I was younger. Younger and stupid. A naïve boy who thought he could have the world. And yet, here was the feeling of déjà vu hitting me in waves as I looked through a list of divorce lawyers. At least, this time, I wasn't planning on selling the house.

Charlotte threw her sippy cup at me, bringing me out of my memories. I grinned at her. The little toothless wonder. I scooped her out of her high chair and headed for the bedroom. "What shall we wear today, Princess?"

Dressed and ready to go, I put Charlotte in her pack n'play so I could get myself ready for the day. I had become so in-tuned with listening for her that it was second nature as I shaved and brushed my teeth, listening to her play and babble. I looked at my reflection in the mirror. There were touches of grey through my hair and some fine lines around the eyes, but overall I didn't look too worse for the wear. If I came through this next divorce unscathed, it would be a miracle. I had no doubt that Madde would not go as quietly as she had last night and I, mentally, geared up for a fight. The one thing I knew she wouldn't fight for would be Charlotte.

A year. The affair had been going on a year. How was it possible that I didn't see any signs? Granted the last six months I had been occupied with Charlotte, but before that. She started six months before Charlotte even came into our lives, before she was even born. About the time the results from the fertility testing came back. How did I not see it? I berated myself, but I knew it was common for spouses to miss the signs of an affair. We had hardly been talking as it was before Charlotte came along. Madde had started working long hours and I attributed it to the stress of finding out we couldn't have kids--correction, that I couldn't have kids. I grimaced. Feelings of letting Madde down and somehow being responsible for Madde's infidelity played through my mind. No. I would not go there. This was not my fault. Love should have been able to overcome this. Would Izzy have cared if we couldn't have kids? I shook my head. Don't go there, dude. Don't go down that 'what if' road, I berated myself.

I threw myself into the job. The divorce process was started and papers had been sent to Madde. So far, she hadn't signed anything and I was waiting for the fight to begin.

I had an appointment to meet with Charles in an hour. Longings for quiet times and smooth sailing pulled at me. There would come a time that it would happen, I knew it

Making the Rules

deep down, but, for now, I wondered when that would be. I stopped by the house to check in with Neil to see the progress he was making on the inside. His contractor was a stickler for details and time constraints. His crew worked feverishly with minimal talking.

"Looks like we may be a little ahead of schedule. Let's hope it stays that way." Neil turned towards me when I came up the walkway.

"That's good." Neil and I ran through the upcoming things that needed to be done. "Okay, I'm off for an appointment. Let me know if you need anything else this afternoon, otherwise, I'll be back in the morning."

I drove through the drive-through at Starbucks to get a coffee. I was a few minutes early and didn't want to sit too long in the car waiting. My mind was a whirl of thoughts as I entered Charles' office. Like usual, he didn't say a word until I settled into a chair.

"Something's changed." Charles remarked.

I met his eyes. Did I really look different? "What do you mean?"

He smiled. "You seem more relaxed."

I nodded. "There have been changes in the past couple of days. A lot of them."

"Do you want to talk about them?"

I thought for a moment before I answered. "The short version is I saw Madde with another man, went home and packed up her things and put them in the driveway. When she arrived home, she took them and told me it had been a year that she had been having an affair. Obviously, Charlotte was not the issue with our marriage."

Charles wrote some notes before he looked up at me. "You don't seem too emotional about it. What are you feeling?"

"At first I was angry when I saw Madde with that guy

and it fueled my packing up her stuff. But now, now I just feel relief. I feel like a cycle has been broken."

"What kind of cycle?"

I closed my eyes for a moment. "A cycle of being stuck in something I didn't want to be in. I know I felt obligated to Madde, but knowing she went outside of the marriage only a year into it and made me feel like bringing home Charlotte was the heart of the matter for our problems, somehow, it's a relief. I'm done with feeling sorry for her and for myself, feeling like I'm always to blame."

Charles sat there silently, waiting for me to continue. I didn't know what else to say. Standing, I crossed the room and looked at his books in the bookcase, trying to focus on titles. "So, you are no longer feeling guilty for bringing Charlotte home?"

I turned. "I never felt guilty for bringing Charlotte home. I felt guilty because I couldn't give Madde a child myself."

Charles nodded. "Ahhh, there it is."

I watched him as I walked back to the chair and sat down. "There what is?"

"The real issue of your obligation, as far as this marriage is concerned."

"And what are the issues with my obligation in other aspects of my life?" I asked, smirking.

"You tell me." Charles countered with a grin.

"So, the reality of it is, my feeling obligated all these years for different things is really my issue. Well, that was easy."

"That's not what I said. You said you had no idea why you felt obligated, at least, in this marriage, so now we know. Your feeling guilty for not being able to have children is not an uncommon thing. Any marriage that has

Making the Rules

one party in that situation, that person is going to feel the brunt of the responsibility, fault, if you will, for it. That's not a bad thing and yet, it is something you needed to realize in order to move forward."

"I just don't understand how she feels no guilt with this. When did it become acceptable to just go outside your marriage vows and be with someone else? If she was that unhappy, just get out. She could have initiated a divorce." Frustration poured out of me and my heart broke at the thought of the last year being a lie in our marriage, before the issues with Charlotte, before my so-called betrayal to Madde by bringing her home. I was the one who had been betrayed.

"People handle things different ways. I know, there should be a semblance of loyalty when it comes to marriage vows. Unfortunately, in today's world, marriage vows aren't taken seriously anymore."

"It doesn't make it right."

Charles shook his head. "No, it doesn't. But you can't change what happened. You can only deal with it and move forward."

"I know. And I'm taking those steps. I'm more involved at work, I started the paperwork for the divorce. I just don't know what else to do."

"All you can do is take it one day at a time." Charles tapped his pen on his notebook. "What seems to be your biggest fear going through this process?"

"Fear?" I sat there thinking. "Other than thinking that Madde is going to do something else that will cause problems, I can't help but think that I'm still the common thread with all these failed marriages or relationships."

"Common thread?" Charles asked. "You can't really say that. Sure, you were the common thread between the two marriages and Isabelle, but there are always outside forces that contribute."

"Maybe." I was skeptical and still felt obligated to take the blame for all of it.

"Don't take this on, Jack. Some things are out of your control and not your fault." Charles' words sounded reasonable, but the tiny voice in the back of my head, the negative one, screamed at me that I was to blame for all of it.

Time ticked by as we sat in silence. Charles watching me. I sat there with thoughts rolling around. Madde--why, why did she have to have an affair? Michelle--It was my fault that I married her for the wrong reasons. Izzy--My heart broke repeatedly every time I thought of it. Why did she push me away?

"Jack." The quiet word broke through my thoughts.

"Yeah?"

"Talk it through. I see the anguish in your face. What are you thinking about right now?"

I shrugged. "I can't help but wonder how any of this happened. Not just with Madde, but, with Izzy."

Charles nodded. "Izzy seems to be the heart of your guilt." It was a statement, simple and straightforward.

"I guess. I've never stopped thinking about her, after all these years. She creeps into my thoughts over the littlest things." My voice trailed off.

"Move forward with the present, but think about Izzy and try to figure out why you are feeling so guilty for the breakup."

"That's it...there was no breakup. I walked away and we just never spoke again. We never verbalized a breakup."

Charles made notes again. "Let's talk about that next time. Jack, remember this isn't your fault. Madde made her choice a year ago."

I nodded and shook his hand. Back in my car, I sat there trying to process the turmoil inside me.

120

twenty

Isabelle

The next week flew by and I threw myself into work to get caught up and, I was hoping, a little bit ahead so I could take the weekend, guilt free, from work. My excitement had grown as I researched the sea turtle nesting and hatching process, and the Emerald Isle area. It was a beautiful spot on the ocean, but October would be off-season so it shouldn't be too crowded. Nick had booked us at a bed and breakfast on the ocean. The anticipation of the upcoming weekend made the last week before the trip seem to drag.

It seemed, if anything could go wrong, it did this week. I had demanded another meeting with graphic designs regarding the book cover for my February release. The first attempt had been awful and I felt like a shrew demanding it be redone, but Gayle was in agreement with me, although she didn't tell me that until we were back in the privacy of her office. She didn't want the cover team to think she was making the decisions, but she had been prepared to demand it be redone if I didn't.

It was Friday afternoon and I was more than ready for these next two hours to go by so I could leave for my mini-vacation with Nick. I walked into the meeting to see three mock ups on easels at the end of the conference room. Gayle had arrived just before and was looking at them. I walked over and studied each one. They were definitely better, but something was still off about them. The colors weren't right. This was a thriller and the colors seemed to cheery. I was expecting darker and more ominous. I glanced at Gayle who was watching my reaction to each one.

"What do you think?" Gayle asked me in a hushed voice so the others couldn't hear. The design team was sitting at the other end of the table waiting for us to turn and address them.

"It's not right. It's too bright and cheery." I sighed.

"You're right. They still have it wrong. Time's getting short though. What are you going to do?"

"I can't put the book out with this. It won't sell properly without the right cover." Frustration coursed through me. "Do we have time to get another round of mock ups?"

Gayle pursed her lips. "They would have to be done on an emergency basis, which means the team needs to be working over the weekend. You need a final answer by mid-week to get it to marketing."

I sighed. I couldn't demand the team work over the weekend if I wasn't going to. Gayle must have read my thoughts.

"You don't have to be here for them to do their job.

Making the Rules

Insist on having another set by Monday. There is nothing you can do over the weekend until they do their job. I know you have plans."

I glanced at her. "I can change them if I have to."

"And I know you would, but it's really unnecessary."

I nodded and turned towards the team. "This isn't acceptable. The colors are too bright and cheery. You've all received the synopsis of the book and been given the specs of what I was looking for. Dark and ominous." I gestured behind me. "This isn't it. I need three new designs available Monday morning to look at."

I heard the groans and looks of disgust, but no one complained. I knew they would do their job and I would reward them for it. "Monday morning, eight a.m. back here. I'm counting on it being right this time." I had become Gayle and dismissed them without saying a word. It was uncanny how my work mannerisms mirrored hers.

"Nice job, Isabelle." Gayle spoke behind me.

"Why do I feel like I'm being too hard on them?" I sank into a chair.

Gayle laughed. "Do you think I have never had those thoughts, especially when I was at the beginning of my career?"

"Really? You thought you were too hard?" I didn't believe it for a second.

"Of course, I did. But I also knew that I had to set the tone if I was to be respected as I climbed the ladder. You command respect, just like I did, and, although they are irritated at having to work the weekend, they also know they didn't do their job. They respect you for making them get it right."

I nodded. "I suppose so."

"I know you. You are feeling a bit guilty at going off

for the weekend and having them work, right?"

"Yeah."

"So you want to show your appreciation to them?"

"Of course. Is that wrong?"

Gayle shook her head. "Use the business credit card and bring them breakfast. I used to do that all the time when I made them work weekends. They respect the demand for perfect work, but they appreciate you even more for rewarding them for their extra time. It is what makes you a good leader, to want to show your appreciation to them. Some bosses would demand the work and never tell them they are appreciated. It separates the tyrants from the leaders."

"Thank you, Gayle."

"Isabelle, you must know and, I probably don't tell you enough, you have incredible talent and have proved your worth in this company. I'm very appreciative to have you by my side, and I can trust you to make the same type of decisions I would."

I glanced at my watch. I had forty-five minutes to wrap things up before leaving. I had arranged to leave by 4:30 so we could, hopefully, arrive at Emerald Isle by eight and get a late dinner there.

"Just get out of here. There isn't anything pressing now that can't wait till Monday. And don't take your laptop with you. Unplug for the weekend." Gayle shooed me towards the door.

"You sure?"

"Absolutely. You have worked hard these past few weeks getting this release together and keeping it on schedule. Go."

"Thanks, Gayle." I scurried back to the office to pick up my things and power down my computer. Heading to

Making the Rules

the car, I sent Nick a text, Out early. Headed home now to grab my bags. We can leave early if you're ready.

I hadn't even turned on the car yet when my phone beeped. I'll meet you at your place in 10 mins.

We would be on the road a good half hour earlier than planned. It was going to be a good weekend. I could feel it in my bones.

It didn't take us long to load up Nick's car with our weekend bags and start off. "You're in charge of tunes." Nick immediately said as he turned onto the main road.

"Oh, good." I rubbed my hands together.

"Don't make me regret that."

"Mwaaahaha." I grinned at him. "Be prepared to rock this car for the next few hours."

Nick laughed and started drumming his fingers on the steering wheel when I turned to the classic rock station. We rode, pretty much, in silence, unless we both were singing poorly with the radio. Laughter would follow the off tune or wrong lyrics and before we knew it, we were turning onto the main road for Emerald Isle.

I was awestruck as we drove into town. The sun was just starting to set and the orange hues glanced off the ocean. I took out my phone, and rolled down the window so I could take pictures. "This is amazing." I turned to Nick. "Thank you."

"For what?"

"For this weekend. This is beautiful."

"Babe, stick with me. This weekend is just beginning." I laughed at his terrible attempt at Bogart.

We found the bed and breakfast and, as Nick went to check us in, I stood on the patio looking out at the ocean. Wow was the only thing I could come up with. It was like I was looking at a different ocean than the one

125

outside my apartment. The colors, the peacefulness…it was just different. I was in love. If I ever moved, it would be to right here.

"It's gorgeous, right?" Nick's voice was right behind me and, as he spoke, he slid his arms around my waist. I leaned back against his chest and sighed.

"I'll run the bags up to the room. You can stay here and enjoy the view. There's a great seafood place that was recommended, just a five-minute walk down the beach."

"I'll help you with the bags."

He kissed my neck. "No, you won't. You'll enjoy the view. I'll be right back."

This was the Nick I could get used to being with. Since we had started planning this trip, he had been loving and attentive, the Nick I had grown to care for deeply before I left for New Hampshire. Grown to care for. That was as deep as I could get. I still didn't believe I loved him, as much as I did 'cared for' him.

"Ready?"

"That didn't take you long." I smiled up at him as he reached for my hand. The walk didn't even seem like five minutes and, before long, the Crab Shack stood before us. There were quite a few cars in the parking lot, considering it was off season. As we entered, we saw the place was near full.

"Two?" The hostess greeted us.

"Yes, please." Nick answered.

"Ever been here before?" She asked as she lead us to a table by the window.

"No, first time." Nick responded.

"You'll love it. We stay busy year-round because the locals think we're the best in town." She winked at us. "Darla will be right with you. I would highly recommend

Making the Rules

the shrimp. No matter what way you get it, you'll love it."

She was gone before either of us could respond. The place was hopping, that was for sure, and was definitely filled with locals. A group was gathered on the other side of the bar where there was a dart board. The bar was standing room only as people stood and talked like old friends who hadn't seen each other in years.

On the side of the restaurant where we sat, were tables and the whole back wall was windows from floor to ceiling giving the view of the ocean to any table in the place. We were fortunate to be sitting right up by the window. The whole place had an atmosphere of home.

"Hi, I'm Darla. What can I get y'all to drink?"

"What's on tap?" Nick asked.

"Our most popular is Ireland's finest, Smithwicks."

"Sounds good to me." I said.

"We'll both have it." Nick answered.

Darla nodded. "I'll be right back with those."

We looked over the menu, but I immediately gravitated towards the shrimp choices. And were there ever choices. Boiled, fried, baked or broiled. Broiled in lemon garlic butter sounded good to me. Probably not very healthy, I told myself, but it was healthier than fried.

Once food was ordered and we were sipping the ale, I found myself people watching. "This is a fascinating place."

Nick laughed. "It feels like home, that's for sure."

"Exactly. Isn't it odd for a restaurant to feel that way? Yet, look at all these people, all acting like they are just one big family." It made me feel a little wistful for the family I wish I'd had. Once the food was placed in front of us, both of us were too busy eating and talking about the incredible food for me to dwell on the longing of a family.

By the time we had finished eating, and Darla offered dessert, I couldn't eat another bite. Thankfully, we had to walk back to the bed and breakfast, and I was hoping I wouldn't feel so full by the time we got back. It was dark out by the time we were ready to go, yet the beach was illuminated by the moon. We walked, taking our time, back to the B&B, hand in hand. As we got closer, Nick stopped me and turned me towards the ocean. Then he wrapped his arms around me.

His warm breath on my neck had me leaning back into him. I wanted to feel his mouth on me and, yet, he just held me. Slowly he opened one of his hands in front of me. In the palm of his hand sat a silver necklace with a starfish charm on it. The starfish was solid and about the size of a quarter.

"Nick, it's beautiful."

He kissed my neck before stepping back to put it on me. As he adjusted the clasp, I reached up to hold the starfish. As he came against me once more, he spoke softly. "I found this when I found the sand dollar. This one has a bit of information with it, too, that I felt was as appropriate as the sand dollar."

"Okay."

"The starfish stands for a period of healing and renewal because they can regenerate healing within themselves. That ability to regenerate is supposed to teach us to trust in our ability to renew ourselves to be a different, but better person." Nick paused. "Izzy, I know things have been hard for both of us, in our past and now, but I want us to be able to heal and renew what is between us."

"That's beautiful, Nick, and you're right. It's very appropriate for us." I turned to him and wrapped my arms around him. "Thank you."

twenty-one

I fiddled with the necklace, the starfish that hung just low enough to reach the top of my cleavage. I fingered the small arms off the body and thought about the meaning behind it. Renew ourselves. It was, indeed, extremely fitting after my trip to New Hampshire, finding out who my mother really was and realizing I still loved Jack. I was renewing myself into a different person, although the jury was still out that I may be a better person.

Nick stood behind me, holding me, but not saying a word. Both of us seemed to be lost in our own thoughts. My thoughts turned to wondering what Nick could be thinking about and if he had secrets from his past that he felt he had to renew himself from. Did the man even have a regret in his life? Did he know what it was like to live with guilt? I wanted to ask him about his lost loved one. Was it someone he had regrets about? Is that why he was so, seemingly, jealous of my memories of Jack? Did he have memories that haunted him day and night like I did?

"You ready to head in?" His voice was soft and low against my neck following the words with soft kisses at the base of my neck, the tender spot that always gave me chills when he kissed me there.

I sighed. "I don't know if I want to leave this view, but yes, I guess it will be here in the morning."

"If I had known this was all it took to get your mind off work, we would have been here a lot sooner." Nick stepped away from me and grabbed my hand. We strolled hand in hand up to the B&B. I turned and took in one last look of the moon sparkling over the water. The waves were mere ripples on the sand with the calmness almost eerie.

I hadn't seen the room yet as I had been admiring the view when Nick brought the bags in. He swung open the door and stepped aside for me to enter. Walking into the room, there was a small wall that jutted out in front of the door causing me to walk to the left of it to enter the room. The wall was the home of the headboard of the bed, which faced the far wall--of windows with French doors opening onto a balcony. They were situated between the rest of the wall covered with ceiling to floor windows. It was the perfect view of the ocean.

I glanced at Nick and he was watching me. "It's gorgeous." I walked over to the French doors and pushed them open. The salt air teased me, beckoning me out on the balcony.

Nick joined me as I leaned against the railing, mesmerized once again by the small waves and the light dancing across them from the moon. I, once again, fin-

Making the Rules

gered the starfish necklace. It was time to let go of the past, of Jack, and start anew. If only that was as easy to do as it was to think it.

"Thank you, Nick." I spoke the words softly, but turned to face him. "For all this."

"You're welcome."

I took a step closer, and wrapped my arms around his waist. I watched him as he pulled me closer and bent his head toward mine. The kiss was soft and gentle. I leaned into him, my hands splayed across his lower back, pulling him closer. I tried to deepen the kiss, yet he pulled away, just a hair, to not allow the kiss to become more than the soft and sensual introduction that it was. I groaned in frustration and Nick pulled back, a smile on his lips.

"We have all night. We don't need to rush." He pulled me closer, but turned his head to look out at the view.

"Seriously, Nick." I tried to pull away from his embrace, but his arms tightened around me.

"What are you in such a hurry for?"

"Not so much a hurry, but let's not drag this out at a snail's pace either." I was irritated, and I couldn't put my finger on why. Was it the primal need for sex, or was it the hope that I would be able to drive Jack from my mind if I gave myself to Nick?

Nick chuckled and pulled me against him. "Izzy." His whisper sent shivers down my spine as he slowly caressed my back while he nibbled my neck. "Relax and enjoy the ride."

I moaned and clung to him. I hated the feeling of needing him this much. It went against my every fiber to need a man like I needed him, physically, right now. The thought pulsed through me...it was just physical. My body relaxed and I released the need to make it more than it was. I went with my instinct and let my physical need guide me. When Nick's mouth claimed mine, I was struggling to hold on to control. His tongue stroked mine and I sucked gently on his tongue. His moan told me I had sent him into more of a hunger that demanded to be met mode than the soft and gentle one.

Never breaking the kiss, Nick guided me back inside until the back of my legs hit the edge of the bed. He slipped my clothes from me as I fought to free him from his clothes. Brushing my hands away, he undressed and pulled me onto the bed with him. Urgency took over and animalistic need pulled us into that moment when no thoughts could break through anything but the need to dull the ache within.

I stretched out beside him in the aftermath of sex. He held me close as my head laid on his chest. Listening to his heartbeat, I tried to find the rhythm with my own, but they didn't sync up. The realization that our hearts were not in sync brought my spirits down. I wanted that...another heart that would beat with mine, be in time with mine, understand mine. It wasn't with Nick, and I had no reason other than the small ones that I seemed to be looking for.

I must have drifted off to sleep fairly quickly. I awoke to the sounds of the waves crashing onto rocks and seagulls calling for breakfast. I glanced over and Nick was still sound asleep. I slipped out of bed, grabbed my clothes, and headed for the shower. When I walked back into the room, Nick had rolled over, but was still sleeping. I scrawled a note stating I was going for a walk and raced out to the beach. Kicking off my flip-flops as I hit the sand, I let my toes sink into the warmth, even though it was still early morning.

I made my way down to the water's edge before turn-

Making the Rules

ing and walking along, allowing the small waves to run over my feet and pull at my ankles as it made its way back out. The water pulling at me pulled the stress out of my body as the ocean worked its magic on me. I walked until I got to the Crab Shack and then turned to head back to the B&B. I hadn't brought my phone and Nick probably would be looking for me.

My thoughts drifted as I walked. Not even realizing what I was doing until a wave hit my knees, I glanced around to see that I had been drifting as I walked and was now walking further out than I had intended. Although my jeans were rolled up, the bottom part from the knees down were soaked. I sighed.

"What are you doing?" Nick's voice behind me broke my attention.

"Getting wet, apparently." I answered, turning to face him as I shrugged.

"On purpose?"

I shook my head. "I wasn't paying attention. I guess I was deeper in thought than I realized. I, evidently, wasn't walking a straight line and walked out a bit further than I intended."

Nick gave me a puzzled look. "And you didn't feel the water?"

"Well, yeah, when it hit my knees." I walked toward him. "Not important. It's just water and I have other clothes."

"I thought maybe you'd want to go into town after we eat and do some sightseeing and, possibly, shopping. I guess things are still open because of the big turtle hatching."

I nodded. "Sounds like a plan. I'll change really quick and meet you in the dining room."

As I entered the dining room, I saw Nick sitting at a

133

table with his plate full. He was drinking his coffee as he looked out the window. However, my attention from the smell wafting through the air, turned towards the buffet. Warm cinnamon rolls, with icing melting off the edges, eggs, bacon, fruit…it all looked so good. My stomach growled in agreement and I heaped a plate high.

Nick laughed when I set my plate down. "There is nothing that stops you from eating, is there?"

"Hey, don't judge me."

He held his hands up in surrender. "I would never."

"Just eat your food. I'll probably still be done before you." I took a bite from the cinnamon roll and sighed. Pure heaven. No words were spoken between Nick and me as we finished our breakfasts.

"You sure you don't want seconds?" Nick chuckled.

"Very funny. I'll be fine until lunch." I grinned at him.

Downtown was a short walk. I felt like I was gawking constantly as we strolled down the sidewalk. The roadway wasn't as busy as I had expected for this, supposedly, momentous event that the town celebrated every year. But, I stood corrected as we turned the corner into what looked like a small street fair. Venders were lined up along the street in tents and people were wandering in and out, browsing. This is where the crowd was.

twenty-two

Jack

Two weeks had passed since I had served Madde with divorce papers. Still, no signed papers had been returned. She was up to something, but I didn't know what. I spent eight to nine hours a day at the new house, working side by side with Neil to keep things on schedule. Cabinets were arriving today.

I pulled up to the house just as the delivery truck pulled away. Neil was in the kitchen opening boxes and making sure everything was as it should be. "These are great, Jack. You need to be the one picking out this stuff all the time."

"Happy to do it. I think they will look great with the countertop." Neil and I spent the next few hours hanging the cabinets. Stepping back and looking at them, I felt a surge of pride go through me. This was the first house in which I had been hands-on for this stuff, and it felt great.

The rest of the day flew by and, by the time I was on the road to pick up Charlotte at my sister's, I was exhausted. The physical work had been a great outlet for stress, but I realized just how little physical work I had done in the past few years. Man, was I sore.

My phone buzzed with a text message as I pulled into my sister's driveway. We need to talk. Madde.

About what?

The divorce papers.

I shook my head. I knew she wouldn't go quietly. What about them? Just sign them.

We need to discuss things. I'm not just signing off on everything. Jack, just meet with me.

Fine. When and where?

Tomorrow. Coffee shop. 9.

I didn't respond, but slipped my phone in my pocket with a sigh. I didn't want to deal with this, but if it was the only way to get her to sign the papers, so be it.

Morning brought a deluge of rain and a cranky Charlotte. She was not happy. Although she didn't seem feverish, the poor child was screaming nonstop. I didn't want to leave her to meet with Madde, but I certainly couldn't take her with me. I called my niece to see if she could come to the house for just an hour to watch her. With her onboard, I was able to settle Charlotte down. I slipped out of the house quietly while she and my niece watched a Disney movie.

I walked into the coffee shop to see Madde seated at a table in the corner. The place wasn't too busy. I sat down across from her and waited.

"Thanks for coming, Jack."

"What's the problem with the papers, Madde? You told me you would just sign them."

"I know, but things have changed. I talked to a lawyer yesterday and we need to change a few things." She wouldn't meet my eyes as I glared at her.

"What things?"

"I want alimony, Jack." She hesitated. "I'm going to need it."

"Why? Your boyfriend can't help out?" I couldn't keep the sarcasm out of my voice.

"It's not that." She took a deep breath and looked up at me. "Jack, please. We are still married."

I stood. "Sign the papers and we won't be."

Madde reached out and grabbed my hand. "Please, Jack. Sit and talk about this."

I slid into the chair, pulling my hand away from hers. "What are we talking about? You want money and I'm not paying you money. You were the unfaithful one in this marriage."

"Yes, I was and I know you are upset, but Jack, we weren't happy."

"That doesn't make it right to do what you did. If you were so unhappy, just get a divorce instead of screwing around behind my back. A year, Madde, we had only been married a year."

"I did love you, Jack. I just wanted a baby so badly."

"And if you had gotten pregnant, what then? Were you going to try and pass it off as my child?"

Madde's eyes dropped and she didn't say a word.

"Shit. You were going to do that. Damn you, Madde. This is done. We are through and you will not get any money from me."

"Jack." Madde's voice was soft. "Please, Jack. Just let me talk."

"No. I'm not listening to another word of this. Sign the papers." I turned to walk away.

"I'm pregnant."

The words froze me. How long had I wanted to hear those words from her? Yet I knew this child wasn't mine. I turned slowly to face her.

"Congrats to you and your lover, but it doesn't change anything, Madde. You have the baby you always wanted, but I'm not involved in that at all. Sign the papers." I turned and was gone before she could say another word.

I sat in my car and dialed my lawyer's number. Before connecting the call, I paused. Eyes closed, I tried to sort through what I was feeling. I wasn't even really upset. Shocked a bit that Madde was holding out for alimony. How would this have played out if I hadn't caught her in the affair? I hung up the phone. I just couldn't think about this right now. I'd deal with it if she didn't send the papers back signed in the next couple of days. If she wanted to fight for alimony, the affair would come out and I wouldn't be quiet about it.

Right now, Charlotte was my only concern. I drove home, shutting Madde's situation from my mind. My poor sick girl needed me and I would be there for her. I would be the best father that girl could have.

I had called to set up an appointment with Charles after Madde's bombshell. I couldn't seem to process what it was that she wanted from me. Money, sure, but Madde had a good job. She couldn't seriously think she could pass this child off as mine since there were medical reports showing that I was unable to have children from about the time she started her affair. It would be very well documented and certainly she was smart enough to know that.

Charles was waiting for me when I arrived. I had no sooner sat down when I stood up again and started pacing the room.

Making the Rules

"Jack, what's going on?"

I stopped pacing for a moment and started again. "Madde's pregnant. She told me she wants alimony." I sat down.

Charles was silent, watching me, just waiting for me to speak.

"Her plan before she got caught having an affair was that, if she got pregnant, she was going to pass it off as ours. Did she really think that would work? Did she think I would assume test results were incorrect? Does she think she can do that now and expect me to pay for another man's child?" Anger was rolling off me now and I couldn't seem to stem the flow of words. "I won't let her. I don't know what to do, but she will not do this to me."

Charles held up his hand to stop the words. "Let's think about this, Jack." The tension in the air filled the room, making it impossible to breathe. I let my head fall into my hands and closed my eyes. Concentrating on taking deep breaths, inhaling and exhaling, I felt some of the tension dissipate. When I looked up, Charles was watching me.

"What do I do?" The question was almost a plea. I had reached my end. Suddenly the stress of everything was too much…Charlotte, being a single parent, working, and now this with Madde…I just couldn't take any more.

"You take a deep breath and deal with one thing at a time."

I growled. "Easy for you to say."

"Of course, it is, but it's not as difficult as you think. Jack, think this through. She doesn't have any way to make you pay for a child that isn't yours." Charles watched me, letting his words sink in. "Have you talked to your lawyer?"

"Not yet. Charlotte was sick yesterday. I just wanted my focus to be on her."

Charles nodded. "And she should be your top priority right now. She's your responsibility. Madde's child is not your responsibility. She was unfaithful and alimony isn't typically awarded when a person is working. If anything, alimony for you could be considered for an award for her unfaithfulness, but, unless you want to drag that through the courts, I wouldn't bother."

"I just want this over with. I want her to sign the papers and for us to be done with each other. She's right. Neither of us was happy. I'm not even upset about the divorce, but I am angry that she wants me to pay for another man's child."

"Wait and see what happens. After that conversation you and she had yesterday, she may just sign the papers." I nodded. Hopefully, she would, but I wasn't going to hold my breath. Charles continued, "let me ask you this. Where have your thoughts been with this?"

"What do you mean?"

"Are you only thinking of Madde or have your thoughts drifted to Isabelle?"

I sighed. Izzy. "I can't say I have been thinking of her all the time, but yeah, she's on my mind no matter what is going on. How different things could have been if I hadn't walked away from her. Or, why did she come to see me and what does that mean for the future?" I paused.

"Let's rephrase that. 'How different things could have been if she hadn't pushed you away'. You need to stop taking the blame."

"I know, but when I think back, we both were to blame. It wasn't all her and it wasn't all me. It was a lack of communication. I should have told her I loved her."

Making the Rules

"Maybe. But she didn't tell you that she loved you. Why think that was all on you?"

I shrugged. "Maybe it would have changed the outcome if she knew how I felt. She wasn't in the best place back then. Her parents didn't make her life easy."

"You don't know for sure what her mindset was. She didn't tell you."

I laughed. "Devil's advocate, huh?"

"The point is, you only know your side, really, so you can't take all the blame for any of what happened back then or what happens now."

Charles was right. I couldn't and I knew that, deep down. But years of being the scapegoat for everything that went on was just a bit hard to overcome. I knew that, for whatever reason Izzy had shown up on my steps, it had triggered a chain reaction that I prayed would lead me back to her.

I awoke with a start when my phone rang. The night had been long with Charlotte up a few times crying. Poor girl was congested with another cold, which, in turn, led to me not sleeping very much. "Hello?"

"Jack, Peter Lawton here. I wanted to discuss the divorce papers if you have a second."

I rubbed my eyes and sat up. "Sure. What's going on? Did she send them back?"

"Not yet. Her lawyer called and wants to talk about you paying alimony."

I sighed. "No. Madde and I met the other day. She wants alimony because she's pregnant. She's not asking for child support because it's not my child and she knows she would never get it. She's been having an affair for a year. If she would like to drag that through the courts, tell

141

them we'll go fight it out. Otherwise, she needs to sign the papers and be done with it."

"Interesting. None of that was conveyed to me by her lawyer. She didn't even mention you two had met."

"Let's get this done, can we?"

"I'll be back in touch." He hung up before I could say anything. I was praying that this phone call would be the last of it and I would just get notice saying the divorce was final. My thoughts were waylaid when Charlotte's cry pierced the room. I stood slowly. My body ached and my head felt as congested as Charlotte's had sounded all night. I didn't have time to get sick.

Charlotte was standing in her crib, eyes red and snot running down her face. I grabbed a tissue and wiped up her face before picking her up and holding her close. "You and me both kiddo." I sat in the rocking chair and rocked her while she snuggled into my shoulder and closed her eyes. I closed my eyes and felt myself being lulled to sleep with the rocking. I dozed off and on as Charlotte snored on my shoulder. I knew, if I laid her down, she would be awake and crying again in no time.

Slowly standing, I went to the kitchen to make some coffee. As it brewed, I took a couple of ibuprofen to ward off a sleep deprivation headache and sent a text to Neil telling him Charlotte was sick and I wouldn't be in today, but would be in contact with the realtor about the open house. A work from home day, hopefully without holding Charlotte all day.

Charlotte had finally gone down for a nap after she had lunch and her decongestant. If I could, at least, get an hour to get some emails done, I would consider it a win. As I sat down at my laptop, and opened my email,

Making the Rules

my heart sank as there was one from Madde. I skipped over it and focused on the work emails. I sent one off to the realtor regarding possible days for an open house and asking her to get some comps to us for the location. After I had finished my work, I sat there staring at my inbox and Madde's name. Finally, deciding to just get it done with, I opened the email.

Jack,

I know things didn't go well the other day between us. But you have to know I still love you and I really don't want the divorce. Please, let's think about what is best for us. We could be a family. Charlotte could have a sibling. Think about it, Jack.

I love you still,

Madde

It was all I could do not to choke. A family? She was thinking of Charlotte having a sibling, when she would only call her "that child" before? She was delusional if she thought she was coming back here to be a family after the crap she had pulled. I forwarded the email to my lawyer with a quick note in the subject line This has to stop.

I opened the internet and did a search on Isabelle LaFayette. I found she worked at a publishing house as an editor. That was about it. Not much on social media, what she did have was private so I couldn't see anything. I assumed the publishing house was in the same area where she lived. Virginia. Why did you come see me, Izzy?

I hadn't told Charles that Izzy had shown up and wondered what he would say about that. We had been so focused in sessions about Madde and this marriage which was very quickly disintegrating.

twenty-three

Isabelle

I was in heaven. I had not spent any time just shopping, or browsing. I enjoyed wandering in and out of the tents, trying on hats and sunglasses. I found a beautiful scarf that fit Diane's personality perfectly and picked it up for a Christmas present. Nick was quiet as he trailed along behind me, never complaining that I stopped at every booth.

As lunch time approached, the crowd thinning out some and, in spite of the fact that my stomach was ready for food, I enjoyed spending more time chatting with the booth owners and looking at things that the smaller crowds afforded. I glanced over at Nick to find him smiling and chatting with one of the owners as I looked through a rack of sweaters.

It was just turning two p.m. when we approached the end of the sidewalk sales. I glanced up as I heard a man call out, "Steve". I looked around and no one seemed to

Making the Rules

be paying attention to the man. He was about my age and was walking towards Nick and me with a smile on his face.

"Steven Melrose, that is you! I haven't seen you in years." He reached out to shake Nick's hand.

A look of rage fleeted across Nick's face. "I'm sorry?"

"Steve, it's me Grayson Caldwell."

Nick looked visibly uncomfortable. I stood back and watched him. "Man, you have the wrong person." He glared at the man before turning towards me and grabbed my elbow. "Let's go."

"I'm not done…" I trailed off as Nick propelled me through the few people standing around.

"Steve?" The man called after us.

"What are you doing?" I tried to pull my elbow out of his vice grip.

His fingers tightened around my arm. "I don't like being bothered by people and that guy obviously has me mixed up with someone else. It didn't look like he was going to let it go." His voice was curt and I glanced up curiously at him. Nick reverted to his behavior of September, irritated and sullen.

"I think that was a bit of a harsh response to him. It was obviously an innocent mistake." I stopped. "Let go of my arm, you're hurting me."

Nick's hand dropped from my arm and he glanced around before looking at me. "Sorry."

"What is going on?"

"God, Izzy, stop being so dramatic. I just was ready to go." Nick turned and started walking away.

I glanced behind me, looking for the man, but he was gone. I walked after Nick, pondering what had just happened. He sulked all through lunch. I tried not to let it bother me, but the more he snapped at me, the more I became irritated and wanted to get away from him.

We walked back to the B&B in silence. My mind raced with possibilities of what had happened. Who was Steven Melrose? Why did this man, what did he say his name was, Grayson Caldwell, think he knew him? Working in the publishing field, my mind immediately ran through mystery book scenarios and, by the time we walked up the steps of the B&B, I had Nick pegged for an ax murderer looking for his next victim. I tried to keep the smile off my face as Nick turned towards me.

"Look, it appears this weekend is ruined. Let's just head back."

I stared at him. "Are you serious? What is going on with you?" Before he could answer, I moved up the steps and into the home. This weekend definitely was ruined and it was Nick's fault. Him and his damned moodiness. I stormed up to our room and started throwing my clothes into my bag. I had my stuff all packed by the time Nick came in. He looked at my packed bag sitting on the bed and didn't say a word.

"Let me know when you're ready to go." I moved to the balcony and shut the French doors behind me. Staring out at the ocean, I couldn't help but think how wrong I was to think I could stay in this relationship. Nick was out of control and I had no idea when it had changed. Did my trip to New Hampshire really bring up so much jealousy in him that he would throw whatever type of relationship we had away?

I kept myself from laughing out loud. Relationship. Yeah, that word was used very loosely. Acceptance of letting myself open up had started to seep into my brain before I left for New Hampshire, but, now…no, there was

Making the Rules

no way I was going to allow myself to be vulnerable to any type of hurt. And at this very moment, Nick was very capable of hurting me. I rubbed my elbow -- physically and emotionally, he could hurt me.

"Ready." Nick's sharp tone drew me out of my thoughts. I nodded at him. The ride home was silent with the radio playing low. There was no singing or laughter. By the time, we pulled up in front of my apartment building, I had a raging headache. Nick started to open his door.

"No, don't get out." I grabbed my bag and slammed the door. Without giving him a backward glance, I walked away from the car. My thoughts had already turned to work and I was mentally preparing to throw myself into my to do list as soon as I walked through my apartment door.

First things first. I started a pot of coffee and grabbed my laptop. I checked work emails and found that the design team had sent me an email just a few minutes ago stating they'd had a good work session that morning and felt I would be happy with the end result by Monday. It stated they would be at work at nine a.m. sharp tomorrow to finish mock ups for me to view. I didn't reply, but instead set my laptop aside and contemplated Gayle's words about showing appreciation to the staff. I knew that I wouldn't be waiting until Monday to bring them breakfast. Tomorrow morning I would be right there with them in the office, breakfast for them in hand for them, to work alongside them and bring this book cover to completion. It felt right to me to be in the office with the others who, on my orders, would be working.

Fresh mug of coffee in hand, I pulled my laptop towards me once again. My fingers tapped on the keyboard as my mind raced with how to go about searching for answers. Could it truly have been mistaken identity with Nick and this man on Emerald Isle? The weight of the starfish necklace around my neck brought my fingers up to touch it. What was prompting all these gifts? Before the New Hampshire trip, Nick hadn't been one to lavish me with gifts. Was he truly courting me as Mary seemed to think?

The pounding in my head intensified and I pushed the laptop aside. Maybe a nap was more what I needed. Glancing at the clock, I realized, maybe it was more food that I needed. It had been a while since lunch and, honestly, I hadn't eaten much after Nick's turn in mood. I made my way to the kitchen and opened the refrigerator door. I really need to do grocery shopping. I shook my head at the meager contents. I had to stop living off coffee and creamer.

I grabbed my phone and sent Diane a text. Dinner?

Yup. Where?

Flamigo's was the usual spot, but I wanted something different. Pete's Pizzeria?

See you in 20. She never ceased to amaze me at how much she could convey in the shortest text. I sent her a thumbs up. The pizzeria was only a couple of blocks away. Walking might help the headache.

I arrived just as Diane was pulling in. "Hey, I thought you were gone for the weekend."

"So did I." I shrugged. "I'll tell you about it over pizza and beer."

For a Saturday night, the place wasn't too terribly packed. We found a small table over in the corner and once the beers were in front of us, Diane gave me an expectant look.

Making the Rules

I shook my head. "I don't know. I'm fed up with his mood swings."

"What happened?" Diane leaned forward to hear over the music playing and the laughter from the dart corner.

I showed her the necklace and told her how great Friday night was. As I continued on to the bizarre behavior at the sidewalk sales, Diane scowled. "Are you hurt?"

"Slight bruise on my elbow, nothing that concerns me." I absently-mindedly rubbed my elbow.

"I have never seen him be anything but charming," Diane said, "but I've never seen him outside of the networking groups either. I guess we just never know people's true personality."

I nodded. "It's like a switch flipped while I was gone."

"Do you think he is truly jealous of Jack or is it something else?"

I didn't speak as the waitress approached our table with the pizza. We served ourselves before I spoke. "I honestly can't say. I do know I don't like the way I feel when he's like this. But I don't know if it's because I just feel different...stronger since I've gotten back."

"Maybe knowing you still love Jack has changed your perspective." It wasn't a question, but a statement. One that I knew, probably, held some truth to it. We switched gears and talked about Diane's love life, or lack thereof, as we finished the pizza. I glanced around the pizzeria and no eligible males seemed to materialize out of nowhere.

"Maybe you need to try a dating site," I suggested.

"No thanks. Do you know the number of creeps who are on those things?" Diane shook her head vehemently.

"More so than the creeps who come across as normal that we run into in person?"

"Probably not, but at least we can pretend that they

are normal until they do something to show us differently."

I wrinkled my nose. "Maybe they are just more truth-
ful behind the screen so we see them for who they really
are immediately."

Diane looked at me. "There may be some truth to
that. It definitely is easier being yourself behind a computer screen than in person." She tipped her beer bottle
at me. "Why don't you go on one?"

"Please. I don't have time for dating and honestly,
after the way Nick's been acting, it will be a long time
before I would want to even consider dating again."

"So what's with the gifts from him lately?" Diane
asked.

"I'm not sure. Mary thinks he's 'courting' me." I made
air quotes with my fingers as I said the word courting.

Diane snickered. "Is that even a thing in our generation?"

"Right," I shrugged. "But the gifts haven't seemed to
fit with the Nick I knew before all this. Now it's almost
like he's trying to buy my affection."

"That's not healthy."

I laughed, "says the life coach."

twenty-four

Isabelle

Sunday morning arrived and I walked into the office, arms laden with bagels, cream cheese and coffee. I found the design team in the conference room, crowded around the table working hard.

"Isabelle." Tom said and stood up when I walked in the door.

"Good morning." I moved to the side table to set everything down. "Breakfast has arrived."

There were choruses of "thanks" as I moved out of the way. As the team filled their plates, I moved over to the table to look at what had been done so far. I liked the improvements. Colors were darker and gave a menacing look to the cover. Although they weren't quite finished, I could tell I was going to be able to approve something today or tomorrow. The ease of working side by side with my team made the day fly by. I gushed over the finished mock ups, which were sensational. They deserved the praise. They had risen to the challenge and spent the time over the weekend making it happen.

I made a decision, but told them I wanted to see them again tomorrow morning to make sure that was what I wanted. As everyone broke up, I cleaned up the conference room, removing any trace of the food that had been devoured.

I sat at my desk going through emails and getting things in order for Monday morning. It was going to be a long day, but I was satisfied with what the team had done over the weekend. It was time to go home and get some rest.

• • •

There was a niggling in the back of my mind. Nick. Why would he be called Steven? Who was this man who ruined my weekend with Nick, or, better yet, why did Nick get so upset if it was just mistaken identity. This was something I wasn't going to be able to put to rest. I reached for my laptop, opened it, and googled Nick Sterling. Nothing. Steven Sterling. Nothing. I shoved the laptop away. Obviously, I had no idea what I was searching for. I flipped on the TV to see if I could find something mindless to take my mind off the weekend.

Perusing channels, I paused on the local news channel, hoping to see the weather for the next day. Breaking News flashed across the screen and a picture of a man who looked similar to Nick appeared. Be on the lookout. Fugitive - Steven Melrose. The words floated across the bottom of the screen. I grabbed my phone and called Diane.

Making the Rules

"Hello?"

"Put Channel 5 on NOW." I stood and listened as the news anchor explained the man had been spotted in Emerald Isle this weekend. He was a fugitive running for the past three years after murdering his wife and another man, thought to be her lover.

"Are you still there?" Diane's voice came through the phone. ·

"Yes." I whispered.

"I'm on my way over." I heard Diane's keys jiggle as she picked them up. "Lock your door and call the cops."

I nodded.

"Izzy?"

"Yes, I got it. Hurry." I disconnected the call and reached for the business card on the end table. Officer Terrell answered on the second ring.

"Office Terrell, Isabelle LaFayette. I had the break-in..."

"I remember. We haven't found the guy yet, and unfortunately..."

"That's not why I'm calling," I interrupted him, "The fugitive, Steven Melrose."

"Yes?"

"I think I have been dating that man, but he goes by a different name."

"Are you home?"

"Yes, sir." I replied.

"Stay there. I'm on my way."

Having hung up the phone, I sat and listened as the news anchor talked about the double murder, how this Steven Melrose apparently found his wife and her lover, and killed them both. They hadn't caught him yet, but had been trying to track him for the past three years. The trail had been cold, but with this new information of a spotting in Emerald Isle, they were asking, once again, for the public to be aware and report anything that might be helpful.

The banging on my door made me jump a mile. "Izzy, it's me, Diane."

I unlocked the door and flung it open. Diane pulled me into a hug as she slammed the door shut with her foot. "Are you okay?"

I nodded and shrugged at the same time. "It certainly explains his behavior when that guy called him Steven."

"Did you call the cops?"

"Yeah. Officer Terrell is on his way here." I had no sooner sat down on the couch when there was a knock on the door. Diane motioned for me to stay still as she went to the door. After peeking through the peep hole, she unlocked and opened the door.

"Isabelle." Officer Terrell walked in and stood in front of me. "Tell me what you know about this man."

I glanced at Diane and she nodded to me.

Taking in a deep breath, I fingered my necklace. "He goes by Nick Sterling. I met him last year and we started dating. However, in the past few months, since I got back from my trip to New Hampshire...when the break-in occurred...he's been different."

He was scribbling in his notebook. "What do you mean, different?"

"More possessive, irritable, flying off the handle at the least little things."

"Did he have a key to your house?" Officer Terrell asked.

"He did, but I honestly never thought about that until he tried to get one day before I got home from work and he said he needed a new key."

Making the Rules

"Did you give him the new key?"

I shook my head. "No, thankfully."

Officer Terrill reread his notes. "I think I have everything for now. Do you have his address?"

I looked at Diane. "I don't. In all the time we have been together, he has always just come here."

Diane put her arm around me. "I don't have it either. He keeps to himself really."

A knock on the door startled me. I started to stand and Officer Terrill gestured for me to sit. He opened the door and let in another police officer who handed him a file. Officer Terrell flipped through it and pulled out a couple of pictures.

"Is this Nick?" He handed me the photograph.

"Yes, but with blond hair, not dark." I handed the picture back.

"I want you to be prepared for this next one. It's not bloody, but just be prepared."

I nodded as I took the picture. I heard Diane inhale sharply. It was like looking at a picture of myself. Same color hair, same color eyes. It was just a head shot but, I would guess her to be about the same build as I am. My hand trembled as I handed the picture back. "Who is that?"

"That's Kristine, his wife."

I closed my eyes. I just wanted this nightmare to end. How on earth could I have gotten mixed up with someone like this, a murderer? My phone buzzed with a text message. I opened my eyes to see Nick's name flash across the screen. "It's him."

Let's talk. Sorry about this weekend. Dinner tomorrow?

Everything in me screamed at me not to do it. I handed the phone to Officer Terrell. He read it and returned the phone to me. "How do you feel about meeting him?"

"I don't want to, not after seeing those news reports and seeing pictures of his wife."

"I don't think you are in any danger unless he knows that you figured out who he is."

Diane cut in. "What are you asking her to do?"

"I'm thinking, if you meet him, we can pick him up at the restaurant."

I stared at him.

"You will be safe the whole time. We will be there in the restaurant and outside." He reassured me. "We will pick him up outside, so you don't even need to go into the restaurant."

"I don't know. How can I even act normal around him?"

"You won't have to interact with him. We'll pick him up just as you get there."

Diane nudged me. "Text him back and set up the dinner."

Ok. Let's meet at Flamigo's. 7?

Ok. I'm sorry about this weekend.

We'll talk tomorrow.

I gave Officer Terrell the information. He assured me they would be there before seven and Nick, or Steven, wouldn't even know they were there. I locked up after I let the officers out and turned toward Diane.

"This is not what I expected at all."

Diane nodded. "I know. I can't believe it. It seems like it is out of some movie or book."

"You don't think he'll try to come here before going to Flamigo's?"

"If he does, you won't know. I think you should come to my place today and stay with me until this is over."

Making the Rules

"Yeah, I think you're right."

I packed up an overnight bag and I followed Diane back to her place. I felt a sense of relief wash over me as she locked the door behind us.

twenty-five

I had been tense all day. After tossing and turning all night, I had, finally, gotten up about four a.m. and made coffee. Diane joined me shortly. I couldn't tell if I had wakened her or if she, truly, hadn't been sleeping either. Coffee on her front porch, watching the sun rise, helped calm the nerves a bit, but the rest of the day, waiting for the time to leave for the restaurant, dragged painfully slow.

I wanted Diane to be able to go with me, but knew she couldn't. My stomach churned with nerves. I was ready to cancel more than once and Diane talked me through the anxiety. I drove slowly to the pier and parked my car. Glancing around, I saw no indication of police cars anywhere. I prayed that Officer Terrell was there. There was no way I would be able to act normal around a man who had killed his wife…a woman who looked eerily like me.

I walked down the pier and saw Nick sitting outside

Making the Rules

of Flamigo's, waiting. Under any other circumstances, I would have been excited to be meeting a man so good looking as he was. The blond hair and blue eyes, along with the lean, tan body, was something any woman could appreciate. Yet, as I moved closer to him, dread filled me and I prayed a cop would show up.

I saw Nick stand when I came into his line of vision and I gave a little wave. I tried to keep a normal pace, but my feet felt heavier with each step I took. When I arrived in front of him, to my surprise, I kept myself neutral when he kissed me on the cheek. He grabbed my hand and opened the door to go inside.

"Let's sit outside" I moved toward the outside seating. We placed drink orders and sat in silence as we waited for the drinks to come.

"Izzy..." Nick started just as the waitress came back with drinks. He paused until the waitress left. "Izzy, I'm so sorry about this weekend."

"Don't you ever get sick of apologizing for this bad behavior?" Suddenly the fear was gone and I was just angry. Mad for the way he was making me feel, mad for taking out his insecurities or anger out on me, mad that I was even in this situation and suddenly wishing I had spoken to Jack when I was in New Hampshire.

I saw a flash of anger on a face before he hid it away. "Bad behavior? Stop treating me like a child."

I took a deep breath. "Then stop acting like one. You were out of control for what reason at Emerald Isle? Because some unknown person mistook you for someone else?"

"And you are always so perfect, Izzy. I wish we all could be as wonderful as you." His words were cold. Fear overtook me again and I wondered if I had pushed it too far. I glanced around and spotted Office Terrill and two other cops walking up the walkway with him. Relief flooded me.

"Not perfect at all, Nick, but I don't use others as a punching bag and I won't be used as one by you." As I stood, I saw Officer Terrill making his way to our table. Nick reached for my hand. "No, Nick. We're through." I pulled my hand away from him and walked away. I passed Office Terrill and stopped at the table.

"Nick Sterling...Steven Melrose, you're under arrest." Office Terrill pulled him to his feet and put cuffs on his wrists.

"For what?" Nick looked at me.

"For the murder of your wife, Kristine Melrose, and Mike Wilson. You do remember them, don't you?" I heard the words and saw the blood drain from Nick's face. He stared at me and I looked back at him. The shock I was feeling was genuine. I knew it was going to happen, but I was surprised at the way it affected me. I heard the blood rushing as my heart pounded. This was real. The realization hit me that, if I'd had this fight with Nick at home, before I knew who he really was, I could have ended up dead, like his wife. My legs buckled as the officers started walking Nick towards the parking lot. I felt the arm of one of the officers around me as he led me to a chair to sit down.

"Ma'am, are you okay?" He asked softly.

I nodded. "I'm fine."

"It's all over now. Do you need a ride home?"

I shook my head no. "I have my car and I live not far from here." I stood just as Diane came rushing over. "What are you doing here?"

"Did you really think I was going to let you do this

Making the Rules

alone? I've been just down the pier waiting for them to get him." She linked her arm with mine. "I've got her, Officer. I'll make sure she gets home safe."

It was over. Nick…Steven, whoever he was, was out of my life for good. Another chapter closed and I had survived another bit of life that would leave me jaded just a bit more. My heart ached as I realized how many times I had survived and how jaded I had become. Jack, I'm so sorry. The moment of truth was, I loved Jack, and, at this particular moment, all I wanted was to be able to lean on him.

For the first time ever I called in sick to work. I told Gayle I would be there tomorrow and then called Mary immediately. I needed some perspective and I knew Mary was the only one who could give it to me.

She fit me in for an emergency session. As soon as I walked through the door, she was all business. "What's going on?"

I started to walk to the window, stopped, and turned back towards the couch. "It's Nick, rather, his name is Steven Melrose."

"Wait, the Steven Melrose who was on the run after killing his wife?"

"You saw the news?"Mary nodded. "Yeah, that's him. All this time and I never knew. But apparently, this is the time of year he actually killed her and, evidently, me going to New Hampshire and looking up Jack triggered the whole 'my wife had an affair' thing in his mind."

"Are you okay?"

"You know, everyone keeps asking me that. I don't know if I'm okay or not. What is okay in this type of situation? What am I supposed to be feeling?" I closed my eyes for a moment to collect my thoughts. "I know I was angry at first, before the cops arrested him. I was so tired of being his punching bag, and, after the cops had him in handcuffs, it hit me that it could have easily been me next who he killed."

"Yes, but you are here and you are safe."

I scoffed. "Safe? What is safe?"

Mary looked at me. "What do you mean what is safe?"

"You make it sound like life is grand now that the 'danger' is gone?" I air quoted danger. "But in reality, I close my eyes at night and I see myself dying at his hands, over and over again. No matter how many times I force myself to wake up, I go back to sleep and it happens again."

Mary took a deep breath. "Yes, that is your mind processing the fear and the reality of what could have happened. You have to keep reminding yourself that it didn't happen and he can't hurt you now. Your mind will, eventually, listen to that and reset to a better mind set."

"Eventually? When will that be?" I stood and started pacing the room. Back and forth, I walked, not saying anything. Finally, I turned toward Mary. "I can't do 'eventually'. I need for all this to stop now." My anger was at a boiling point. I had had enough. I wanted my life back, but what life? I wanted a life with Jack. I always had and now, more than ever, the loss of what could have been between us was more real and prominent than ever before.

"Whoa. I know you want things at a normal level, whatever that is for you, but when you go through a trauma and, yes, this was a trauma, you have to work through it and process it before things get back to that level."

"That's just it. I threw what could have been a good life away and, for what? For crap to happen time and time

Making the Rules

again to me? When does it stop?"

"When you stop it." Mary's words were soft, but direct.

"How?" The anger had subsided and I sat back down to listen.

"You have to come to the point where you are not going to let your life circumstances dictate your life. You have a good life, Isabelle. You have a great job, great friends and, yet, you are fixated on Jack. Why is that?"

"I didn't say anything about Jack." I protested.

"You didn't have to. When you say you threw away a good life, you mean your chance of a life with Jack. It happened. Life happens. Why are you holding onto that still?"

"Are you telling me to let it go?" I challenged her.

Mary smiled. "I'm telling you to decide what you want for your life and make it happen. Let go of what could have been and make what you want to be, happen."

I shook my head. "It can't happen."

"Why?"

"Jack has a family now."

"Ahhh, Jack was holding a baby so you came to the conclusion that he has a family. Do you know for sure it was his child? Do you know for sure he is married?" Mary already knew the answers to those questions, so I scowled at her. "Izzy, decide what you want. Forget Nick. You didn't love him anyway, and now he is out of your life."

I didn't love him. I had known that I would never love him, and the truth was, the more he had pushed lately, the more it had turned me off and I wanted less and less to do with him. Mary's voice broke through my thoughts. "Go to work tomorrow, Isabelle. Make some priorities in your life for what you really want, whether they include Jack or not, and start taking those steps to make them happen, whatever they are."

twenty-six

Jack

I felt like time had sped up in the past few months. Charlotte was growing like a weed, pulling herself up and cruising a bit around the furniture. Being a single parent had moments when it was a bit easier as we found our routine between work, day care and home life; but then there were other moments, when I was completely overwhelmed, wondering how I could get myself through the next few years, at least.

I pulled up to my sister's. It was common practice for Charlotte and me to have dinner at my sister's most nights. Not only did it help me, but I think my sister enjoyed it just as much. I walked into the kitchen with Charlotte playing on the floor and my sister cooking. She glanced up at me and, immediately, I knew something was wrong.

"What's going on?" I asked her as I kneeled to kiss Charlotte.

Making the Rules

"Not much." She turned back to the stove.

"Not much? Come on, give me some credit for knowing you better than that."

She motioned to the table. As I set plates out and got Charlotte settled into her high chair, she put the food on the table. We filled our plates and I prepared a plate for Charlotte. As we started to eat, I waited for my sister to speak.

"I ran into Isabelle's grandmother today. You remember her?"

"Grams…" I smiled. "I certainly do." I had such fond memories of those few weeks Isabelle and I were together. Grams was Izzy's world. "And?"

"She was talking about how hard Izzy has had it lately."

"What do you mean?"

"Look, Jack, I'm only telling you this because I know how you feel about her and I never would say anything if she hadn't showed up at your door." My sister spoke fast as she watched me.

"Spit it out, Sis."

"She was dating a guy who was just arrested for killing his wife three years ago."

"What? Is she okay?" My stomach clenched at the thought of something happening to Izzy.

"She is. She was instrumental in getting him arrested, actually. Her grandmother is worried about her, but you know how it is when you love someone."

I heard her words, but my thoughts were on Izzy.

"Jack?"

"Yeah."

"Did you hear me?"

I stared at her. "Yeah, Grams is worried about her."

She smiled a little and then started laughing. "Your wheels are spinning, thinking about Izzy and how you want to comfort her, aren't they?"

"No." The word came out sharply and we both knew I protested too much because, that was exactly what I wanted to do.

We ate in silence. I cleaned Charlotte up and got ready to head for home to get her to bed. My sister walked us to the door, and as I opened it to leave, her question stopped me in my tracks. "What are you going to do?" I didn't have to ask her about what. I knew what she was asking.

I started to shrug, but then looked her straight in the eyes. "I'm going to go talk with Grams." She nodded.

After getting Charlotte in bed, I sat in the darkened living room and thought about what my sister had told me. Izzy. After all this time, I wanted to really make a difference for her.

I approached Grams' house and stopped just shy of the door. I wasn't sure of what kind of welcome I would get and here I stood with Charlotte in my arms. I took a deep breath and rang the doorbell. The door opened and there she stood, Grams. The woman hadn't changed a bit in the past years.

She grinned at me. "Jack, you get yourself right in here. Look at that little one."

"Hi Grams." I gave her a kiss on the cheek as she hugged me tight.

"It's about time you came around. All these years and you are still as handsome as ever."

I felt my face redden. Grams never did mince words. She reached for Charlotte, and Charlotte was happy to go to her. I followed them into the living room as Grams sat down and was chatting with Charlotte, who was lis-

Making the Rules

tening intently while keeping one eye on me. I glanced around the room. Nothing had changed since the last time I had been there. My memories overtook me as I thought of the last time I had been in that room. It had been December 26th, two days before I took Izzy to the base. We had stopped by because Izzy was more at home here than at her parents'. I had felt as welcome then as I did now.

"Well, Jack, this one is just a delight. Your sister mentioned the circumstances in which you came to have given this child a home."

"Thanks, Grams. She keeps me going every day, that's for sure."

Grams laughed. "I imagine she would." She paused for a moment, watching me. "I figured you would be coming to see me, or, rather, I hoped you would be, after I told your sister about Izzy."

"Is she okay, really okay?" I sat forward in my chair.

Grams nodded. "You know Izzy. She's a survivor."

"Yes, she is, but she shouldn't be just surviving."

Grams put Charlotte on the floor with some old cardboard spindle cones from the old weaving factory and Charlotte entertained herself with putting them on and off each other. Then Grams looked at me, "You two know better than anyone what it is like to survive heartache."

"What…?" I started.

"Don't question it. I know Izzy went to see you when she was home."

I couldn't deny it. Grams knew already, but I didn't know why. Maybe she did. "Why, Grams? Why did she come to see me?"

"Are you asking why because you didn't want to see

her and she upset your life, or are you asking why because you need to know where her heart is?"

I thought. I wasn't upset that Izzy had come to see me, but I did need to know where her heart was. "I think you already know the answer to that." I smiled as she nodded.

"Jack, Izzy has never been one to be able to acknowledge her feelings very well, verbally. She hides herself away to protect herself."

"But, I thought…"

Grams cut in. "You thought you had done something wrong and that's why she pushed you away?"

"Yes."

"This is a conversation you need to have with her. Didn't you talk when she was here?"

I sat back. Grams didn't know Izzy hadn't talked with me. Why hadn't Izzy told her that she turned and walked away? "We didn't talk, Grams. We didn't have the chance."

Grams just nodded and mumbled, "Well, that explains so much." I didn't question her. She wasn't truly speaking to me, but to herself and I had no idea what she was talking about. I waited to see if she would fill me in.

"I can't stay long, Grams. I just needed to know if Izzy was okay."

"She says she's okay." Grams was noncommittal. "Let me get you and Charlotte some of those chocolate chip cookies you used to love so much. Got a batch made just this morning."

I picked up the few toys Charlotte had been playing with while I waited for Grams to come back. We met her at the front door and she handed me a container with the cookies in it. I hugged her close after taking the cookies. "Thanks, Grams."

Making the Rules

"You bring that cute little thing back to see me again. You know you are welcome here anytime, Jack."

"Thanks." I smiled and turned to go out the door. Grams placed her hand on my arm and I turned towards her.

"Jack, our girl needs you." She let go of my arm and I just nodded. As I buckled Charlotte into her car seat, my mind kept repeating her words, our girl needs you. Did Izzy still care for me? Grams must know something I don't, or was it just the fact that I showed up here that Grams could see how I felt. I was torn, but I knew what I had to do.

As Charlotte drifted off to sleep as we drove down the road, I reached for a cookie. Opening the container and pulling a cookie out, I noticed a piece of paper tucked inside. I pulled it out and saw Izzy's telephone number and address on it. I love you, Grams. That woman had more insight than anyone I knew. I was going to go get our girl.

I called my sister on the way home from Grams to tell her about my plans and she agreed to take Charlotte for a few days. When I got home and, after getting Charlotte down, I started the process of looking for flights to Virginia. With Grams note, I wanted to just go there. I didn't want to call. I had to see her face to face.

With a flight booked for the next afternoon, I packed my bag and a bag for Charlotte for her stay with my sister. I didn't sleep a wink and when morning arrived, I was in the kitchen drinking coffee, just waiting for Charlotte to wake up. I was ready to get to the airport, even if my flight didn't leave for another six hours.

I didn't think about Izzy's reaction to seeing me. I only thought of the pain and hurt she must be going through, and how much I wanted to be there for her. The truth hit me hard. I still loved her. It didn't matter how many years it had been, I still loved her.

As soon as Charlotte woke up, and breakfast was eaten, and she was ready to start the day, I packed up the car and drove to my sister's. Expecting us, she met us at the door. "Are you sure this is what you want to do?"

"Not a doubt in my mind. I have to do this." I hadn't told her about the conversation with Grams in detail only that Grams had said Izzy was okay.

"What did Grams say?" My sister pushed.

"She told me to go get our girl." I looked at her and waited.

"Our girl? Well, well, that certainly puts a different light on it, doesn't it?" I just grinned at her and knew I had her full support. I kissed Charlotte goodbye. As much as I needed to be with Izzy, it was not going to be easy to leave that sweet little girl, and I prayed that she would be good for my sister and not cry too much.

The time waiting for the flight was pure torture. By leaving at 12:30, it would be 4:30 pm before I got to Virginia. On the first leg of the flight I sat back and started thinking back to the day Izzy knocked on my door. Charlotte had spit up on me, and Izzy just turned and walked away. I couldn't imagine what was going through her mind, although, through my mind ran the question of why was she there, and the thought that she looked so good. I turned my mind to the last time I had seen Izzy before that.

It had been that day in the mall, the day she pushed me away and I walked away from her. I turned my back on her and just walked away. There had been no fight, no break up. We just stopped talking. For all this time, I had wondered what I had done wrong. Had I pushed her that night at the barracks?

Making the Rules

We landed in Baltimore and changed planes. As I sat back for the last leg of the flight, my mind turned to that fateful day of December 28th. It was my fondest memory of Izzy. She was so shy, and yet so determined that she wanted to give herself to me. The gift she had given me. I have never taken that lightly. I loved her more than I ever thought was possible that day I made love to her. It wasn't about sex for me. I just wanted her to feel the love I had for her, to be as intimate as possible and show her what could be between us. Yet, somehow, I had failed to show her that.

In the aftermath of our love making, she had lain with her head on my chest, saying she never wanted that moment to end. I had thought, at that time, we were feeling the same, love for one another that could withstand anything. Yet, the very next time I saw her she pushed me away. The hurt from that day I had carried with me every day all these years, until I saw her on my doorstep. I forgot the hurt the moment I saw her and felt nothing but love for her again. I never had stopped loving her.

As the pilot announced the descent into the Virginia Airport, my anxiety level ratcheted up a notch. What if she shut the door in my face? What if she didn't want to see me? What was I doing on this flight? I knew deep down I needed to see her, yet fear laid heavy on my chest...fear of the unknown. Would she be happy to see me? Why did she really come to New Hampshire? To see me? Why? The universal question that no one ever seems to get an answer for.

I only had my carry on, so debarking from the plane, I was able to head right for a taxi. Giving the driver Izzy's address, I sat back and tried to relax. The twenty-minute ride had my stomach churning. My hands were clammy and I felt like I was going on a first date as a teenager. I was ready to turn around and head back to New Hampshire, but the need to see Izzy and make sure she was alright pushed me down the path to her home.

I stood outside her apartment complex and took a deep breath. The salt water smell from the ocean had me turning towards the beach across the street and just listening to the waves for a moment. This was so Izzy. The sound of the waves, the smell of the ocean. She always talked of how these things relaxed her. I took in the sound and scent around me. Inhaling deeply, I found the courage to walk up the stairs to her apartment. Standing at her door, I knocked.

twenty-seven

Isabelle

The late afternoon sky was ribboned with reds and oranges as the sun started its descent. I had just hung up the phone with Officer Terrell telling me Nick, or Steven, admitted to trashing my apartment. A sense of relief washed through me and I was caught up in watching the sky change color when a knock at the door startled me. I froze for a moment before I consciously reminded myself that Nick was gone from my life. I stood and walked to the door. Peeking through the peep hole, I could see the back of a man. There was something familiar about him, but I couldn't see him clearly.

I opened the door and Jack turned to face me. "Izzy."

"Jack." The word left my mouth, but my mind was screaming what the hell are you doing here. We stared at each other for a moment. "Why are you here?"

Jack gave me a tentative smile. "I thought we should

continue the conversation that didn't happen on my doorstep."

I couldn't help but start laughing. "How about a walk on the beach for that conversation?" I reached for his bag. "We can leave this here. Give me a second to get my keys." He nodded and stood outside the door, never making a move to step inside. That gave me a bit of comfort, and memories of how he had always been a gentleman came flooding back. I paused when I reached for my keys. How could I explain to him why I had gone to his house? Did I even know why myself?

I grabbed the keys, locked the door, and we walked across to the beach. Kicking off my sandals, I carried them as we started walking down the beach. Jack walked a few steps before stopping to remove his shoes and socks to walk barefoot with me. We walked in silence for a few minutes. I had no idea where to start and waited for him to say something. I glanced at him and he seemed to be struggling with what to say.

"How did you find me, Jack?" I kept my voice quiet, partly as it was a question for him, but, in part, I was asking myself.

"Grams."

I stopped. "Grams told you where to find me?"

He nodded. "I went to see her when I heard about what happened with the guy you were dating."

"Nick…Steven. Whatever his name was, yeah, that was a real doozy to deal with." I tried to laugh it off, but I couldn't yet laugh about it. And, yet, it didn't make sense why Jack went to see Grams. "I don't understand though. How did you know about it? And why go see Grams?"

Jack stopped and faced the water, standing ankle deep in it, the waves gently lapping at his feet. I stood

Making the Rules

next to him, waiting for his answer. "Izzy, I was worried. Grams ran into my sister and told her what happened, she told me and I went to see Grams."

"You were worried?" I glanced up at him. He hadn't changed much in all these years. A little older looking, but, God, he was handsome.

"Why are you surprised by that?" He turned to face me. "Just because you pushed me away didn't mean I stopped caring about you." Frustration laced his words.

"Wait...I pushed you away?" I tried to joke, but felt the defenses go up to protect my heart and struggled to keep from getting defensive.

"Izzy, why did you come to my house while you were in New Hampshire?"

I searched Jack's eyes. He was sincere. There was no judgement lurking. He genuinely wanted to know why I was there. I shook my head. "I don't know, Jack. I just wanted, needed..." My words trailed off and I looked down at the waves.

"Izzy, talk to me." His voice was soft.

"Jack," I glanced up. "I needed to apologize."

"For what?"

"I didn't mean for things to end the way they did. I never meant to hurt you and I know I did. And I handled things so badly." The words tumbled out of me and I tried to stop talking before I said something I would regret. I closed my eyes, humiliation washing over me.

"Izzy, we both handled things badly. All these years, I thought I had done something wrong. I believed you thought I forced you that day at the barracks."

"Oh, my God, Jack, no, of course not. I wanted that just as much as you." I felt heat rise to my cheeks as I heard my own words.

Jack reached for my hand and laced his fingers with mine. "Izzy, there are so many things that were never said."

I looked at our hands intertwined and looked up at him. Those blue eyes, eyes I had never forgotten, looking down at me. "Jack, that day was the best day of my life. You have to know that."

He smiled. "I hope so. It certainly was for me."

I turned back to watch the sun dipping down to be even with the ocean line. Jack stood beside me watching it, too. Hand in hand, we watched it sink slowly into the horizon. As the sky darkened, I felt a sense of hope course through me.

"Where are you staying tonight?" I asked him.

"I haven't thought that far ahead. I booked my flight yesterday and here I am."

"Let's go back to the house and talk." We turned back towards the way we had come, and walked in silence until we got back to the apartment. I hesitated for just a second at the door, reminding myself again that this was Jack, not Nick, and I had nothing to fear from him.

I opened the door and he followed me. After locking the door, I turned towards him. "Something to drink? Coffee, wine, beer?"

"Whatever you are having." He replied.

"Really? Do you drink wine or would you prefer a beer?" I quirked an eyebrow at him.

"A beer, please."

I gestured for him to sit and went to the kitchen. Pouring a glass of wine for myself, and opening a beer for him, I took a deep breath and waited just a second before returning to the living room. We sat at the opposite ends of the couch, facing each other. I sipped my wine, watching him.

Making the Rules

"Izzy, what happened?"

I didn't have to ask when. I knew he was talking about all the years ago when I pushed him away. "I…" I shook my head and took another sip of my wine. He waited patiently for me to continue. "I didn't know how to handle things. There was so much you didn't know then, and I was afraid to tell you."

"Tell me now."

I took a deep breath. "Shortly before we met, while still at college, I tried to kill myself." I held my hand up as Jack started to speak. "Let me just say it, please. I was young, had felt for years like I didn't belong in my own family. I just couldn't deal with the loneliness anymore, always feeling like I could do nothing right."

"How, Izzy?" Jack asked. No judgement, just concern laced his words.

"Pills and alcohol." I took a drink of my wine. "I was brought home and wasn't allowed to go back to school. Then I met you…and everything changed."

"Izzy." Jack pulled me close to him and just held me. "I wish you had told me."

"The suicide attempt, the way my parents treated me, you, that day at the barracks. I guess I just didn't know how to handle it all." It sounded lame even to me.

"That day, Izzy, at the barracks…how did you feel then? Were you not happy?"

"I was happy. Happier than you will ever know. It was the best day of my life. I felt…in sync with you. I never wanted that day to end."

Jack frowned. "I don't understand then. What changed in those few days that you pushed me away? I know I said the wrong things…I never meant to make you feel I had an obligation…"

"It wasn't you, Jack. Please, know that. Obligation, yes, threw me, but it was everything else in my life. After the suicide attempt, I felt I had no right to be happy. My mother made me feel that way. Jack, you made me happy. I felt I had to give you up because I didn't deserve you."

"Oh, my God, Izzy. You deserved every bit of happiness, then and now." Jack put his beer aside and moved down the couch until he was right next to me. He pulled me close into his arms and I melted against him. "I wish I had known. Izzy, I would have fought to make sure you stayed happy."

Hearing those words, that he would have fought for me, broke the damn inside me. Tears filled my eyes and I allowed the emotions to overcome me. I held him close and allowed myself to grieve those years, all those years that we let slip by us because of my stupidity.

"Izzy." He pulled back to look at my tear-stained face. "Don't cry, Izzy. I never wanted you unhappy."

"I'm not unhappy. There have been so many missed opportunities between us. That is what I grieve the most. The 'what ifs', the lost moments."

He nodded. "I know." His head dipped down and his lips met mine. It was a gentle kiss, non-demanding, yet wanting more. I opened to him, and allowed his tongue to tease mine. He pulled back and watched me.

"Jack, why did you come here?"

"I told you, I needed to see that you were okay after hearing about everything."

I smiled up at him. "I'm sure, if Grams gave you my address, she gave you my number, too. You could have called."

"Yes, I could have, but I needed to see you. I wanted to talk to you when you were in New Hampshire, on my doorstep, but you just left. Why didn't you say anything?"

"You had a baby."

Making the Rules

"Well, not personally."

I watched him break into a smile and I just shook my head. The tension broke a bit more. "Okay, you, personally, didn't have a baby. Who was that darling child who spit up all over you?"

Jack sighed. "That would be Charlotte. And yes, she is my child, but not like you think. My niece's friend gave birth to her and couldn't take care of her. I agreed to take her in and be her guardian. She wanted me to adopt her, but I said I would wait a year before making the adoption final, just in case she changed her mind. Charlotte is now nine months old and, honestly, I can't imagine giving her up. I want to adopt her, but I will stick to the one-year agreement. If she decides she wants her back, it will break my heart, but I will honor that agreement."

My heart exploded hearing him talk. He was the father I knew he would always be. I could hear the love and pride in his voice as he talked about Charlotte.

"That day you showed up, Charlotte had been sick and still wasn't feeling well. I had been getting spit up on quite a bit for a few days."

"I didn't know what to say. I just assumed you were married, with a child, and I didn't want to interfere."

Jack nodded. "In total honesty, I was married. Madde, my wife, didn't want anything to do with Charlotte. I couldn't figure out why she was so resentful towards her, but I can't have children and Madde wanted a child so bad…her child though, no one else's. We are divorcing now, though. She has been having an affair for a year, long before Charlotte came into our lives, and, I just recently found out, she is pregnant now."

I listened careful to his words, and a twinge of sadness

hit me about his divorce, but also my brain was screaming in joy. "So what happens now?"

"With us?" Jack asked.

"With your marriage, and Charlotte? She is your priority." I knew that was the case, and I didn't want him to deny it, but I wanted there to be room for me, too, possibly.

"The marriage is over. There is no chance for reconciliation because I don't want one. Charlotte, well, she's with me for the rest of the year and, if her mom decides she truly doesn't want her, then I will move ahead with the adoption."

"As a single parent?"

Jack nodded. "It's not easy, but I wouldn't change having Charlotte in my life for anything."

This was the man I had always dreamed would be in my life. The man I knew Jack would be all those years ago. In my gut, I had known Jack would be a great father, and I still imagine a great husband.

"What about you, Izzy?" Jack watched me. "What happens now, with you, after this ordeal with…Nick, was it?"

I nodded. "I move on. Hey, I have survived before, I'll survive now." I fell back into my flippant attitude, the one that kept anyone from seeing how I truly felt.

Jack stared at me, seeing through the charade, and, with a quiet voice he asked, "And how are you really?"

I blinked back tears. This man sitting in front of me was the man I always knew, the one who, even when I was eighteen made me feel alive. After all that I had been through, he was next to me, concerned about me. No judgement about the situation I had been involved in, no judgement about my life at all…just concern. Shit, I can't break down in front of him. I prided myself on never crying in front of anyone, and yet, as hard as I tried to stop the flow of tears, I could feel them coming.

twenty-eight

I tried to stand. I just needed to get to the other room. I couldn't let Jack see me cry. I didn't want to be temperamental, that girl who cried over every little thing, yet just having Jack next to me, heightened everything I was feeling. He grabbed my hand as I started to stand, and pulled me back, next to him.

"Don't run, Izzy. Talk to me."

I shook my head, "I just need a moment."

He pulled me close. "Take your moment, right here next to me, but don't walk away."

I felt his need for me to stay with him...or fear of me leaving. Did we both have that fear from the last time we were together? Fear of being vulnerable in front of him paralyzed me. My body was screaming to get away from him, to hide away in the bathroom have my cry and then fix my make-up so he would never know. But, as his fingers laced with mine and his thumb made small circles on the top of my hand, I softened. The walls started dropping and with them dropping, the oncoming tears built up inside of me. I wouldn't be able to stop them. All those years of protecting my heart, and, with one evening talking with Jack, everything I had fought so hard to build up came crashing down.

The tears flowed down my face, and I sat there holding Jack's hand, my face turned away. Eyes closed. He didn't say a word. He let me have my moment, just holding my hand. After a few moments, he pulled me closer to him, wrapping me into his strong embrace. I couldn't help myself, I turned and buried my head into his chest. I couldn't stem the tears and, yet, he said nothing. His gentle strength coming through in the way he held me, just letting me process what was happening.

"Izzy, you're a survivor, more so than you ever realized. All those years ago, you had no idea how strong you really were after surviving the suicide attempt, and surviving the way your parents treated you. You survived, again and again, and made your life worthwhile. You will survive this, too, but I want to be right here for you."

After a few moments, the tears slowed and I looked up at him. "Oh, Izzy. I didn't want you to cry." He let go of my hand and, his hands almost caressing my face, he wiped the tears away.

"It's not…I just…" I had no words and yet he nodded.

"It's been so long, and so much has happened."

I nodded. My thoughts raced. He was sitting here in front of me and I had no idea what tomorrow would bring, but for this moment, right here, we had today and I wanted the most of it. I couldn't waste the time with tears. I wanted that second chance with Jack, even if it was just for today.

"Jack." It came out a whisper, but as I looked into his eyes, I knew we were at the same point, wanting the same thing.

Making the Rules

His lips claimed mine with urgency. He was demanding and I met him with my own demands. As our tongues teased each other's, our hands roamed over each other's bodies. I couldn't get enough and the barrier of clothes between us spurred me to stand, pulling him with me. I walked backward to the bedroom, our kisses never ceasing, stopping only long enough to rid ourselves of our clothes.

Kissing me softly on the lips, suckling my bottom lip into his mouth, he gently teased my nipples, rolling them between his fingers. I moaned softly, my fingernails lightly trailing up and down his back. Jack kissed down my neck, finding that sweet spot between my neck and shoulder. I whispered his name, as memories of that first time flooded back to me. The tenderness he had demonstrated that day so long ago mirrored the tenderness he showed me now. His mouth moved lower until he captured my peaked nipple. I arched my back, wanting more.

I wanted him now, I didn't want this slow build. The need in me for Jack had been building for the past eight years and I couldn't take the anticipation any longer. "Jack, please."

He chuckled and did not increase his pace at all, as he moved to my other breast and gave it the attention I desired. Moving his hand slowly down my body, his fingers found my wetness and I cried out as he teased me. His thumb circling my clit just enough to drive me to the edge, but not push me over yet. My body ached and I moved to try to increase the pressure. He gave in to me for just a few moments, but as I reached the crest he pulled back leaving me gasping for more.

This is what I had been missing all these years. What if I hadn't walked away? Would this heat between us have remained all this time? At this moment in time, it no longer mattered. He was here and this is what I had been wanting. All those nights sitting and remembering him, wishing things had gone different. This was the moment for redemption.

He moved back up and found my lips with his, the kiss teasing and challenging. I reached for him and stroked him gently until he was moaning for more. I gave him the same torture he had given me, teasing him to near climax and then releasing my grip. We both were on the edge and couldn't wait anymore. Animalistic instinct kicked in. As Jack entered me, I felt a sense of home hitting me. The feeling that I finally found where I should have been all along. With every thrust, my defenses crumbled and my realization of how strong my love was for Jack increased. We moved in complete harmony with each other, tumbling over the crest together as one.

As Jack moved to my side and pulled me close, I laid my head on his chest. And, just as before, his heart was, once again, beating in sync with mine.

epilogue

"But what happened then, Grams? Momma didn't go to Virginia with Papa."

I smiled at Nikki. She was the perfect image of her mother, Charlotte, and the apple of her grandfather's eye. Jack couldn't adore this little girl more, nor could I. "No, your momma stayed in New Hampshire while Papa came to see me."

This was a familiar story that I had told and retold many times to our granddaughter. She was a sucker, even at such a young age, for the ultimate romance. Jack and I definitely had the ultimate romance. "When did momma meet you?"

"Papa brought your momma to meet me a few weeks later. He still lived in New Hampshire and we had to see each other only every few weeks for a while." My mind went back to the day Jack left for the airport. I had been terrified he would never come back and my heart ached at the thought of him walking out of my life again. I had tried so hard to not show my tears to him, but he knew my anguish and comforted me the best he could. In reality, I found out later, he had the same fears I did. The art of walking away was a trigger for sad and heartbreaking memories.

I sighed. Texts had been sent back and forth constantly during the days we were apart and then, suddenly, Jack was back at my side, with Charlotte. I had fallen in love, instantly, with her. And, with Jack as a father, my heart couldn't have been any fuller.

"Grams…tell me more." Nikki pleaded.

"About what?" She had been sitting on the floor in front of me, and immediately jumped up and crawled into my lap.

"'Bout you and Papa, and momma." This girl never got enough of hearing it.

"Papa brought your momma to meet me. Your momma was such a happy baby, much like you. Always smiling and laughing. She adored Papa and it was obvious that she didn't want to be away from him. But I think, eventually, she learned to like me, too."

"Momma loves you, Grams." Nikki laughed. It was the same thing every time. And Nikki was right. Charlotte had taken to me almost immediately.

"Papa and I saw each other as much as possible, but going back and forth from New Hampshire to Virginia was hard. I decided it was time for me to start working at home and I left my job at the office."

"The job where you picked books to go to the stores."

"Yes, something like that. I loved my job, but I loved your Papa more and wanted to be there for him and your

Making the Rules

Momma." Leaving my job had been the hardest decision to make. That job had given me hope when I needed it, and freedom from my past, to a point. It was my starting point to what, I thought, was going to be a new life. Never had I thought that my life would end up going full circle and I would be back where I started, with Jack. Oh, the obstacles we had endured over the years, both of us apart, and somehow, we found our way back to each other with a love that was stronger than ever.

"Grams...more." Nikki's plea broke through my thoughts.

"About the time your momma had her first birthday, Papa asked me to marry him. I was in New Hampshire visiting and we had gone to walk on the beach. Papa dropped down on one knee right there in the wet sand, at the edge of the waves and asked me to marry him."

"Did you love him?" Nikki clapped her hands.

"I loved him with all my heart and I had for years. Of course, I said yes." Nikki grinned at me. She knew this story and wouldn't let me give any other answer.

"What happened next, Grams?"

"We got married the next year, right there on the beach where Papa proposed. Just me, Papa and Charlotte."

"You married Momma, too?"

I thought back to that day. "Yes, I did. I married your Momma, too. We wrote our own vows. In my vows, I promised to, not only love your Papa forever, but to love your Momma like she was my own."

"That's when Momma got to start calling you Momma."

I nodded. "Yes, that's when I became Momma to Charlotte."

"What about Auntie Sarah?"

"Auntie Sarah came to live with us a few years

later when your Momma was four." Sarah had been a year old when we adopted her. I hadn't been a part of the first years of both of my daughters lives, but it didn't matter. Those girls were in my heart, as if I had given birth to them myself. It never was a thought of not wanting to adopt. Jack had told me that he couldn't have children and how Charlotte came to be in his life. The fact that Jack had the capacity to love a child who needed a home just deepened my love for him. I never gave it a thought that I wouldn't carry Jack's child because, as far as I was concerned, we had our children together. The moment they were placed in our arms, those girls were ours, both coming to us through different paths, but ours, nonetheless.

"Where did Auntie Sarah get her name?" Nikki asked.

I shook my head. "You know this."

"Tell me."

"Auntie Sarah was named after my Momma."

"My Great Grams?"

"Yes, Nikki. Your Great Grams. I never knew her. She died when I was a baby. But see that picture over there? That's a picture of your Great Grams with your Gigi."

"I know Gigi." Nikki nodded seriously.

"Yes, you do. Gigi is my Grams."

"What happened next?" She was insistent about this story. Needing to hear it to the very end.

"And they lived happily ever after." Jack's voice came from the doorway. Nikki giggled and ran to be picked up. Jack picked her up and swung her around. "Princess Nikki, don't you know this story by heart?"

"Yup, Papa. But Grams tells it so good. It's my favorite." Nikki was so serious.

"Did Grams tell you how much I loved her and how

Making the Rules

I couldn't wait for her to move home to be with me and your Momma?"

Nikki nodded. "She says all the time how much you love her. Grams says you are her reason for living."

Jack smiled. "And she's mine."

about the author

Emma Leigh Reed moved to Tennessee after living in New Hampshire all her life. She has fond memories of the Maine coastline and incorporates the ocean into all her books. She has three grown children and is enjoying her empty nest. Her life has been touched and changed by her son's autism - she views life through a very different lens than before he was born. Growing up as an avid reader, it was only natural for Emma Leigh to turn to creating the stories for others to enjoy. Emma Leigh continues to learn through her children's strength and abilities that pushes her to go outside her comfort zone on a regular basis. She is the author of romantic suspense, women's fiction and has co-authored children's books. She shares her love for writing as an English Professor at a local community college.

emmaleighreed.com

ENJOY AN EXCERPT FROM
A FINE LINE
BY EMMA LEIGH REED

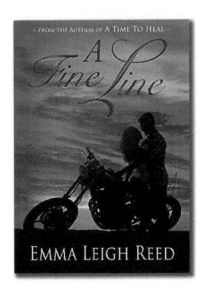

AVAILABLE IN PAPERBACK,
KINDLE, AND AUDIOBOOK!

available wherever you
buy your books

CHAPTER ONE

Grace McAllister glanced around the crowded room. She knew she looked the perfect grieving daughter dressed in a conservative black dress and black pumps. Her long brown hair was pulled back into a sleek bun. She was grieving, but this isn't the way she wanted to be doing it. Her mother, Abigail McAllister, had been very popular in this small town. She ran many committees in town and her hand had been involved in all that had gone on from making sure people down on their luck had food on their pantry shelves, or helping people perfect their resumes in looking for a job.

Abigail had been the epitome of what a small town should be—people helping others and taking care of their own. Although Grace had agreed with everything Abigail had stood for, she couldn't help but shake that there was more to life than this. She wanted more.

Grace sat, back straight, hands folded in her lap, her eyes downcast as the minister droned on and on about her mother's attributes. Grace was grateful for the life she had known growing up. They hadn't lacked anything and Grace had opportunities that most kids just didn't get unless they were of the wealthy class. She cringed. She hated that people still associated her with the wealthy class. She had wanted to do more, and had insisted that Abigail not give her anything else, but allows her to live on her own. Grace had completed her degree in elementary education and loved her job as a second grade teacher. She made a decent living and loved her one bedroom apartment that paled in comparison to her childhood home.

The last song started and Grace stood with the rest of the congregation paying their respects. She pasted on her smile saved for these occasions, and greeted the town people coming through saying condolences. She nodded and smiled. Her cheeks ached and Grace wished more than anything she could head home and slip into a hot bath. Her feet were killing her. She wanted to kick off the dreaded shoes and go barefoot. Abigail would understand, she knew Grace's preference for bare feet that had followed her through childhood into her adult life

She hesitated a brief moment as a man standing a few people back made eye contact with her. He was dressed in a leather jacket and jeans. His dark eyes were the color of dark chocolate, pulling her attention to him. She cleared her throat and glanced back at Abigail's elderly neighbor, trying to focus on what she was saying.

"Thank you, Mrs. Smythe, for coming. I know you will miss mom."

Grace smiled and nodded through one more person before the handsome man in leather stood before her. His grip on her hand warmed her to the core, heat flooding her face.

"I'm sorry for your loss." His deep voice, kept low just for her ears, flamed the fire starting within her.

"How did you know my mother?" Abigail tried to slide her hand out of his, but he kept his grip.

"I, personally, haven't seen her in years. But I'm here out of respect for my parents who knew her." He smiled and squeezed her hand before letting go.

"Wait." Grace reached out, laying her hand on his arm. "Who are your parents?"

He patted her hand. "I'm not sure you would know them." Before she could respond, he had moved out towards the door. Grace inwardly groaned in frustration. She didn't know who he was, and who his parents were.

She continued, nodding, making the appropriate comments as the line continued. She sat down as everyone left the church and headed next door to the fellowship hall for some food. The town's Women's Auxiliary had prepared a feast in honor of Abigail who would have normally been the one in charge of these types of deals. Grace sighed. She just wanted to go home and put this all behind her.

"Everything okay, Gracie?"

Grace glanced up and saw Reverend Sawyer. "Yes, sir. Thank you. You did a beautiful job today. Mom would have been so pleased."

"Everyone loved her and will miss her greatly." Reverend Sawyer held out his hand to her. "Don't you think you should go next door and mingle with those who are here for you?"

"Of course." Grace stood and smoothed her wrinkleless dress into place. "Thank you again."

Grace screamed internally. She still was made to feel two years old, being told what to do. My God, she was a grown woman of twenty-five. Couldn't she decide if she wanted to mingle with people or just go home? She could hear her mom now. Gracie, shoulders back. Never let people see you're upset. Be strong and do the right thing. She was so tired of doing the right thing.

Entering the fellowship hall, she found not as many people had stayed as she had feared. Finding a clear path to the coffee, she made her way there. It was slow progress as people stopped her, sharing stories of her mother. Finally, reaching the coffee, she reached for a cup. Her hand stilled when she heard the voices. "She'll be just fine. She's a good girl. Never was in a bit of trouble."

Grace poured her coffee. She held it as she closed her eyes. Always the good girl. God, she hated that phrase.

"Going to sleep?" The familiar deep voice brought her eyes open wide as she turned towards him.

"No. But it would be nice if I knew who you were."

"My apologies. I guess I forgot to introduce myself. Xander."

"Xander...?" Grace waited.

"Just Xander."

"I'm glad you came. Although it might have been a bit more appropriate to dress in other than a leather jacket and jeans." Grace bit her bottom lip. Her mother would have killed her for sounding like such a snob.

Xander's deep laughter brought a smile to her lips. "It probably would have and I apologize for my appearance. See I just got into town this morning, just moments before the service started. It was either going to change and be late for the service, or show up on time like this. I felt this was the lesser of the two inappropriate behaviors."

"A man who is on time. That is definitely a positive attribute to have."

Xander placed his hand under her elbow, and led her to a quiet corner. "I have a feeling you would rather be somewhere else."

Grace looked around the room. This was her hometown, her family in every sense as these people had watched her grow up, had supported her through tough teenage times, when her dad died and shared her victories when she graduated high school and college. How could she resent being here? She turned towards Xander. "What makes you say that?"

Xander sipped his coffee, keeping eye contact.

"A hunch. I think the 'good girl' may not want to play that part right now."

"Play a part? What are you talking about?"

Grace pondered his words. He was right. She wanted to do something spontaneous and forget who she really was—whoever that may be. "I can see it in your eyes, beautiful eyes by the way. You want to shrink away from these people and be anywhere but here. Can't say I blame you. Funerals give me the creeps. I would prefer to pay my respects to someone I love in a way that they know would be unique for only me."

"Kind of hard to do that when you held to a higher expectation by everyone around you."

Xander nodded. "Screw expectations. They always fall short anyway."

She tried to stop it, but the giggling bubbled up inside of her and escaped. Grace covered her mouth with her hand. Gaining control, she glanced at Xander. Amusement radiated across his face, his eyes twinkling.

"Now that's a beautiful sound, Grace."

She shook her head. "It's inappropriate to be laughing like that at my mother's funeral."

"Why? Did Abigail never hear you laugh?" He scowled. "I bet she loved hearing that sound from you, and would love it on a day like today of all days. You laughing, remembering your mom for the woman you knew her as, not the one that everyone else saw."

Grace smiled. "She was a different person at home. You know, she used to dance around the kitchen and sing. Of course, she couldn't carry a tune if her life depended on it, but how she loved to sing." Grace stared into her coffee cup. The image of her mom dancing with her dad in front of Grace. Grace had loved seeing the love shine from both of them. It was like she wasn't even there when they were in each other's arms. Her mom had always told her Never pass up a chance to dance with the man of your dreams, Gracie. It's like heaven on earth.

"See. Remember her for what she was to you, Grace. Not to everyone else." Xander took her empty cup. She stood there watching him walk to the trash can to throw out the cups. His jeans fit snugly and the muscles rippled beneath them. She wished his jacket was off so she could see the rest of him.

"You ready to get out of here?"

"I can't go, Xander. I need to stay while people are here." She shook her head slowly.

"Wait right here." Xander wandered off. Grace watched him corner Mrs. Smythe and speak to her. She nodded her head and waved to Grace.

"Let's go. You have permission from Mrs. Smythe."

"What did you say to her?" Grace quizzed him.

"Just that you were tired and I was going to make sure you got home." Xander again placed his hand gently under her elbow and led her from the room. Once outside, Grace stopped and took in a deep breath.

"Thank you. I don't know how you did it, but thank you."

"I did nothing. You want a ride home?"

Grace glanced around and the only unknown vehicle in the parking lot was a motorcycle. "On that?"

"Yeah." Xander smiled. "I have an extra helmet."

"Ummm, no. I'll walk. It was nice to meet you though, Xander." Grace hesitated. "Who were your parents again?"

"I don't believe I said." Xander smiled and turned towards the motorcycle. "You sure you don't want a ride."

"No, thank you."

"You've never ridden one before, have you?"

Grace's face flushed red. "No."

Xander stepped close to her. "I won't let anything happen to you. Let your hair down and hold on to me if you're scared."

Grace met his eyes. "I'm not scared."

"I'm thinking you are, but you probably aren't 'dressed appropriately' anyway."

Grace's eyes widened. Xander's mouth twitched as he tried to hold in the laughter. Her laughter mixed with his as she punched him in the shoulder. "Go, wise guy."

She turned towards home and started walking away, thoughts running through her mind of Xander and his motorcycle. She would love to ride that motorcycle with him, her arms wrapped around his waist, head against his back. She sighed. It would never happen. Nice girls didn't ride motorcycles. She made a mental note to ask Mrs. Smythe if she knew his family. Xander was a mystery, one she hoped was just passing through town. She couldn't afford to be sidetracked from all she had to do now that Abigail was gone.

Ever the perfectionist, Abigail had made Grace a list of exactly what needed to be done. There was going to be a meeting with the lawyer, and then of course, Abigail had insisted that Grace move back into her childhood home. Grace shuddered at the thought. She loved her one bedroom apartment and had no desire to move back into the mansion that lay on 72 acres of sprawling farm land. Abigail had wanted horses, but before making that decision, the cancer diagnosis had come through and everything changed. Abigail's focus suddenly became on fighting the cancer and putting her affairs in order. One of the things she had made Grace promise her was that she would fill the barns with horses. Grace had no desire to have horses and wondered how much Abigail would haunt her if she reneged on that promise.

Grace let herself into her apartment, leaning against the closed door. The darkness filled the room. Grace at that moment, couldn't find any positive elements in today or what the next few months, let alone years might hold for her.

EXCERPT ©2015 BY EMMA LEIGH REED
& ELR PUBLISHING. ALL RIGHTS RESERVED.

ALSO AVAILABLE FROM
EMMA LEIGH REED

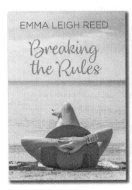 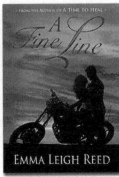 

 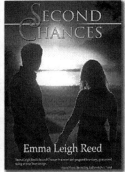 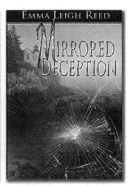

available wherever you buy your books

Made in the USA
Columbia, SC
24 December 2019

85644437R00115